THE DOLL ROOM

THE DOLL ROOM

And Other Stories

CLAIRE L. FISHBACK

ISBN: 978-1-970121-09-4 (eBook)
ISBN: 978-1-970121-10-0 (eBook)
ISBN: 978-1-970121-11-7 (Paperback)
ISBN: 978-1-970121-14-8 (Paperback)

Library of Congress Control Number: 2020918527

This is a work of fiction. Any references to historical events, real people, or real places are used fictitiously. Names, characters, and places are products of the author's imagination.

Cover image by Amanda Keil
Cover Design by Claire L. Fishback
Cover Layout by Steven Novak

Printed in the United States of America.
First edition. October 1, 2020.

Dark Doorways Press, LLC
PO Box 620514
Littleon, CO 80162

info@darkdoorwayspress.com
DarkDoorwaysPress.com

For you, dear reader. This one's for you.

Contents

Introduction

We can all agree that 2020 massively affected everyone in the entire world. Some more than others. My 2020 started out with a bang—literally. On January 9th, I hit my head, suffering my fourth concussion. We wouldn't know how much damage my brain had suffered until August. It took a bad neural stimulation treatment to lift the proverbial veil.

The compounding damage from four concussions had affected deep regions of my brain. My flight/fight region was active all the time, leaving me in a constant state of high stress, with little ability to control my anger. My reward/pleasure zone was inactive, making it difficult to do much, because what was the point? I felt no sense of accomplishment. Areas of my brain responsible for regulating my mood were damaged. I could only feel melancholy and an overpowering sense of ennui. I was drowning in sadness.

My prefrontal cortex had to seek help from other, under-qualified regions of my brain to perform most functions. This slowed processing speeds, made it difficult to find words and make decisions, let alone switching quickly between tasks.

As I write this, I am having what I refer to as a Good Brain Day. Nothing has set me off in a Hulk-Smash kind of way, and nothing has overwhelmed me to the point of paralysis and tears.

Finishing this book, as you can probably discern, was a feat of miracles.

It was originally inspired by a conversation I had with my twin sister, Melissa (whom I call Wissa), in 2019. The original title was "The Room with All the Doors." I wanted to show one story premise presented in different ways. I wrote a failure of a story first, followed by "Changing the Shapes." Then I took a break and worked on something else. Then I hit my head.

Since I had limited screen time during the first couple of months of recovery, I wrote by hand. The first story I wrote with my concussed brain was "The Doll Room," and thus, the title of this collection changed.

But I still wanted to prove that one story premise can have many outcomes. An actual room in a creepy little house my husband and I stayed in for my birthday in 2018 inspired the stories.

The little house was red with white trim, like a barn. It had a small kitchen, a living room, two bedrooms, and a bathroom. The best part was a set of stairs leading to a second-floor attic area. The steps were decoupaged in old yellowed newspapers. Sadly, they were advertisements, not articles about murders.

Tiny doors lined the walls of that weird room at the top of the stairs. Latches or hooks kept a few of them closed. Others had little beds blocking them. I regret not taking more pictures.

I only looked behind two of the doors. Inside was pure

darkness. Having a healthy fear of the unknown, I promptly slammed the cupboards and relatched them.

What else could be behind those doors? What could come of those who dare explore them more than I had the guts to? What madness lies within? Read on to find out.

Claire L. Fishback

Morrison, CO

August 2020, in the time of COVID-19

The Doll Room

My grandma had a huge doll collection. Dolls of various sizes, ages, and materials. Porcelain, cloth, plastic. She even had a few vintage Barbie Dolls on stands with their cat-eye makeup and coiffed hair, a collection of Kewpie dolls grinning from one corner of the room, and an array of Cabbage Patch dolls old enough to have yarn hair from another. The dolls wore a broad array of clothing, too. Victorian dresses, modern skirts and blouses, nighties, clothing for every era or occasion. They were all arranged on shelves in one room of her expansive house where she and my grandpa raised my mom and my four uncles.

My uncles had no interest in the doll room. Living on the acreage they did, the boys were always outside playing in the woods. Since my mom was four, she always wanted to play with her older brothers. They always said no, so she stopped asking and found interest in the dolls. She wanted to play with them, but Grandma wouldn't let her.

And you know how that goes for kids—and most adults, really—say, "no, you can't," and the thing the kid can't do instantly becomes the most coveted and desirable.

There was one doll in particular. It was a baby with an over-sized head. A bonnet covered its porcelain skull.

The baby had big blue eyes that remained open in a fixed stare. It wasn't like a usual baby doll. Instead of a soft body with plastic appendages attached, a cold hard material made up her body. Ceramic or porcelain.

The baby wore a nightgown closed at the neck with two snaps. The sleeves were short and puffed at the shoulders. She didn't have hair, but there was the suggestion of hair, like a Kewpie doll. Light brown paint, airbrushed on, peeked out from under the edge of the bonnet's lace and curled down onto her forehead.

She had big cheeks and a little pink mouth. I think she was supposed to look like a real baby, but the material forming her head and body was too rigid to provide necessary details, like a nose with nostrils. Her nose was a bump in the middle of her face. The bonnet hid most of her head. I didn't know if she had ears and, by the time I saw what was under that bonnet, I was too horrified to pay attention to whether or not she did.

It happened a few years ago, and to this day I can't stand the sight of dolls. Heaven forbid I ever have any daughters of my own.

It was mid-summer. Grandma had passed away. She'd been sick for a while, so it wasn't a surprise or anything. My mom asked me to help her out at the house. Her plan was to clean it out, clean it up, and move in, even though it was far too big for a single person. I've always been close to my mom. I know the real reason she wanted me there was for support. Because of the doll room.

Mom told me about the times she tried to play with the dolls, and the one time grandma caught her with the baby, about to take her bonnet off. Grandma had rushed in and removed the baby from Mom's hands with slow movements reserved for catching small animals.

"What have I told you about being in this room?" Grandma asked with the baby safely in her arms. Mom said she had fire in her eyes that did not match her gentle tone.

"What have I told you?"

Mom said the low calmness of her words coupled with the look in her eyes made Grandma that much scarier. Mom backed out of the room, and as she went, she heard Grandma mutter, "Never take the bonnet off. Never take it off." She hummed an unfamiliar lullaby and settled the doll back in her bassinet.

When Mom was ten, she developed an aversion to that room. She told me what had happened on the fourth day in that house.

We made excellent progress in the other bedrooms leading up to that day. I could tell Mom was avoiding the doll room at all costs. She kept her eyes averted whenever she walked past with another bag full of donations or trash.

Mom came back to her brother Bobby's room—not sure why *they* couldn't help clean out their own crap—and I asked her.

"Mom ... why do you avoid the doll room?"

"What? Avoid?" She laughed. "I don't avoid it." She brushed my question off with a wave of her hand.

"Every time you walk past it, you look down at the floor or at the blank wall across from the doorway." I felt a little bad calling her out like that.

Her lips pulled into a tight line, and she touched my arm. "Let's go outside for some air," she said in a quiet voice.

We went out onto the wide front porch and sat on the

bottom step.

"Remember how I told you the story about the baby in there?" Mom asked.

"Yeah. Grandma told you to never take her bonnet off," I said.

Mom shook her head and let out a long sigh. "She didn't tell me that. Not directly anyway." Mom looked out over the circular driveway to a stand of aspens clustered at the center. Tears filled her eyes. "I took her bonnet off." She blinked and a tear fell. "Grandma caught me with the doll after I already put it back on. I'm sorry I didn't tell you the truth before."

"What was under it?" I asked. There had to be a reason she couldn't take it off, right?

Mom shook her head. "That doesn't matter," she said. "But after I took it off … from that day on … I could hear —*can* hear—the baby crying. Even now." She whispered the last two words. Tears slid down both cheeks. She stared forward, still for a few seconds before visibly shaking herself and smiling at me. She didn't wipe away the tears almost like she didn't realize they were there.

"Why don't you go finish up in Uncle Bobby's room for me?" she asked. "I'll be up in a sec." She brushed her hand down my arm and squeezed my hand.

I nodded. "Okay. Sure."

Back upstairs, I paused in the doorway to the doll room and surveyed the shelves and floor where dolls stood, packed shoulder to shoulder. I half expected them to all turn their heads at the same time to look back at me. In the center of the back wall was the white bassinet, grayed with age and dust.

I crept forward, as if there was a live baby in there I didn't want to awaken, and peered down into the lacy bunting.

Her glossy face peered up at me. I reached down and pulled the silk ribbon at her throat. The lace around her face loosened. I slid the bonnet off over her forehead and down the crown of her head.

Mom's story had me freaked a little. Instead of just rolling her over, face down on the tiny mattress and light pink blankets, I lifted her.

Her body was hard and cold. I turned her over when mom gasped behind me.

I dropped the baby as I whirled around, eyes wide. My mom's eyes seemed to watch the baby fall. She reached out a hand but snatched it back to cover her face when the porcelain hit the hardwood floor and shattered. I closed my eyes. A musty smell rose from the floor.

"Don't look," she said in a horrified and shrieky voice. "Don't look."

I had to look.

A strange wheezing sound came from my mom. But I had to look.

Among the shards of broken porcelain and dust was a shriveled brown form with an oversized head. It curled in on itself, tiny limbs held tight against its malformed body. I backed away and hit a shelf with my shoulder. A few dolls tumbled down around me. I screamed and ran to my mom, leaping over the busted figure. She held onto me, then hauled me down the hallway by the hand, gasping and spluttering.

At the bottom of the porch steps, she kept going until we reached her car. We got inside.

"What the hell was that?" I asked.

Mom looked up at the window to the doll room through the windshield and back at me.

"My sister," she said with a sob. "It's my sister."

That was when the crying started.

Broken/Beautiful

For Belle, October 2005–June 2019

The air for the past few days has been thick and unable to fill my lungs completely. She notices. We lay together every morning and breathe together. She takes me to the doctor twice, and after the second time, she is so sad. She cries from her heart. Throwing herself on me and promising me things. Promising to not let me suffer. Promising to love me forever.

The air grows thicker. She holds me tight against her, telling me it'll be okay, crying heart's tears. They drip onto me. I press my head against her belly, trying to breathe the thick air and her scent. My body is rigid. I can't relax into her like I used to.

She holds my head. She holds my paws. I'm reminded of those moments when we napped together. Me in her arms, holding hands. My paws in hers.

. . .

The pain slips away. The air loses its thickness. I can still hear her whispering how much she loves me. How much she'll miss me. I feel her hands stroking my ears. Her lips kissing my face. I smell her hands by my snout. She wants me to know she's still there, and I do. I know.

I'm called back home. Great white feathered wings flap at my sides, lifting me up and up and up. I see her hugging me one last time. Stroking my ears. Smoothing her thumbs over my closed eyes.

I watch her. I see her touch the paw print they gave her and the wooden box she placed my collar on. I see her gaze to my favorite place on the couch, and I know she knows I'm watching her and loving her even from afar. And I know she keeps her promise of always loving me.

I watch her heart heal with the joy from the new pup I selected for her. The cracks and holes in her heart filling in with loving light. Held together with gold, filling the holes and cracks. Her heart will never look the same. It will always have the marks of our life together etched into it, filled with golden love.

Broken and beautiful.

A Year After Your Death

A year after your death, I finally learned what love truly is. You kept me from it for so long. Told me what you wanted me to believe. A year after your death, I'm finally free of you and your jealousy of the other men in my life. But you still haunt me in moments when I slip into my old ways of thinking. The fear and panic return. A year after your death, I find myself happy—most of the time. You kept me from that, too. I can't blame you, no matter how hard I try. Misery became comfortable. It was my life. Our life. A year after your death, and I still smile on that day. Sometimes I forget and wonder where you are, what you're doing, what other women you have belittled, mentally abused, made dependent upon you. I merely look out at the yard at the slowly sinking mound where you are buried, and I remember.

Changing the Shapes

Inside her head, Saundra had a room with six little doors lining the walls, three on each side. It was shaped like an attic, and in the center was a small table and chairs with a potted flower. She called it her decision-making room, because whenever she needed to make an important decision, she could visit the room and crawl through one of the doors to live out what would happen if she chose that option. If the outcome was a Game-Over scenario, she tried the other door to investigate other outcomes. It all took a matter of seconds, though she could be in the room for hours, or even—with choosing to marry her husband— a lifetime.

It was how she learned that if she had kids, one of them would die at fifteen leaving his twin brother alone and bereft and depressed enough to commit suicide, leaving Saundra and Harvey to a grief that would tear their marriage apart.

She had this ability long enough to know the doors showed the truth. Predetermined fates, parallel universes.

She didn't know how it worked but she—so far—had lived the life the first door on the left had shown her when she said yes to Harvey. And she knew—since she decided not to have kids—that she and Harvey would live happily together well into their nineties and they would travel the world together.

Control belonged to Saundra.

Until the day she didn't know what to do.

Life had been so black and white until that day. Option A or Option B? Even though there were six doors in the room, she only ever had two to choose from. When she arrived, the first doors on the left and right showed her options with little gold plaques.

Marry Harvey. Don't marry Harvey.

Have kids. Don't have kids.

Dye hair blonde. Don't dye hair blonde.

Simple yes or no decisions. Easy. The doors showed her what her life would be, which gave her the info needed to make an informed choice.

She even used the room for minor decisions, like buying a new dishwasher. Model 2 would leak all over their newly remodeled kitchen and ruin the teak hardwood floor, resulting in costly restoration. She went with Model 1, which would not cause those issues and would faithfully clean their dishes for decades to come.

It never occurred to her to even wonder why there were more than two doors. Three on each side of the room.

But then something changed.

Harvey got into a horrible accident, leaving him in a coma.

This was not in the plan. This was not part of the life she saw when she chose, *I Do*. This was not supposed to happen. She bawled these words over his comatose body.

She stumbled out of his room on weak knees, groping at the wall to orient herself in this new world. This world without the Harvey she saw a lifetime with.

The doctor was in the hallway.

"Does he have an advanced directive?" the doctor asked in a quiet voice.

Saundra shook her head. They were young! She just turned forty and Harvey was only forty-two.

"I'm sorry to tell you, as his spouse, you'll need to make some decisions on his behalf."

"Decisions?" Saundra wiped a tear from her cheek and brightened. She could make decisions. Oh yes, she could!

But before any decisions could be made, Harvey died.

It happened so fast. There wasn't even time to say goodbye.

She visited the room with all the doors, looking for answers.

Why did this happen when the doors had shown her a full life of travel and happiness until their nineties? It never showed her an early and untimely death.

When she closed her eyes and went to the room, however, the doors were all blank. No golden plaques with options. When she opened them, infinite darkness stared back.

"Hello?" she shouted into one of them. Her voice echoed and echoed forever.

She slammed the doors so hard a couple of them bounced back open. She sat at the table and put her face in her hands to cry before remembering she was inside her mind.

The potted flower had died.

Saundra looked around for a watering can to revive the dry, brittle, lifeless flower. When she couldn't find one, she threw the pot against the wall. Frustratingly, the clay pot did not break.

One of the other doors opened. One at the back she had never used.

A woman with short blonde hair crawled through. Saundra recognized it as a haircut she had considered years ago and decided against. A decision that was made before she met Harvey. When the woman got to her feet, Saundra took a few steps back.

It was her. Only this Saundra looked both younger and older at the same time. Her face had a few more wrinkles and was a shade darker with a tan.

"Oh, hi," blonde Saundra said with a floppy wave of her hand. She tucked the longer front of her hair behind her ear. The cut was adorable. So was the blonde.

Saundra tugged on a strand of her long dark hair before flipping it over her shoulder.

"Who are you?" she asked.

Blonde Saundra pointed to her hair.

"I'm the Hair Decision. You can call me Blondie," she said with a grin. "I don't think I've seen you here before. Which one are you?"

"I-I'm sorry?"

Blondie nodded. Her eyes closed in what Saundra knew was her understanding face.

"This is the first time you've seen one of us, isn't it?"

Saundra nodded.

"Something bad happened then," Blondie said.

Saundra nodded again. "M-my … our? … husband—Harvey—died."

Blondie shook her head. "Not *our* husband," she said. "I never married."

"You decided not to marry Harvey?"

Blondie shook her head again. "I never even met him."

Saundra opened her mouth, brow furrowed in confusion. Blondie touched her arm and motioned to the table and chairs. Saundra took the nearest chair and sat. Blondie picked up the potted flower, scooped the dirt back into the unbroken pot, and placed it on the table.

"I'm sorry about your husband," she said.

Saundra bit her lips and looked at her wedding ring. "We were supposed to be together into our nineties," she said. A tear dribbled down her cheek.

Blondie nodded and gripped Saundra's hand.

"That's the shit end of the shovel, isn't it?" she said. "I was supposed to have fifteen years with Old Blue. She decided to chase a bunny into the street." Blondie saddened. "Best fucking dog ever."

Blondie used language Saundra never would.

Another door opened, and another Saundra, one with white strands shot through her dark hair, crawled inside. Blondie gave her a little wave once she stood upright and brushed off the knees of her jeans.

"Hey, Kiddo. Good to see you." They hugged. Blondie pointed to Saundra. "This is the Husband Decision." She pointed at this new Saundra. "Husband Decision, this is Kiddo." She rolled her eyes, seemingly at herself. "The decision to have kids."

Saundra nodded in understanding.

"Kiddo's boys both died," Blondie said.

"I know," Saundra said. "I saw … I saw that and decided not to have them."

Kiddo sat in the third chair. "I'm the by-product of that decision." She gave Saundra a grim, close-lipped smile. "They were the best boys. I wouldn't trade the time I had with them for anything."

"How … How's Harvey?" Saundra asked.

Kiddo scoffed. "That son of a bitch left me when I got pregnant."

That wasn't how Saundra saw that life play out.

"No … what? But … he was there for the soccer championship, and the spelling bees, and the science fairs, and-and when they died … right?"

Blondie and Kiddo exchanged a knowing glance.

"She doesn't know?" Kiddo asked.

"Doesn't know what?" Saundra asked, looking between the two who were also her, yet so different.

"The doors only show *possible* outcomes," Blondie said. "We can't control the decisions the other people in our lives make. Those decisions shape the storyline, for lack of a better word."

Kiddo nodded in agreement at the word.

"Kiddo couldn't control Ben's decision to get in a car with a drunk friend, and she couldn't control Tyler's decision to take his own life out of grief."

"And Blondie couldn't control Old Blue's decision to run into the street after that bunny."

"Fucking bunny," Blondie spat. "I hate them all."

"And I," Saundra said in a dazed voice. "I couldn't control Harvey's decision to take the route home over that old bridge." She missed him. He'd only been gone for mere hours and god did she miss him.

"Grief shapes us," Blondie said. "You can't live a full life without it, because it would mean you never loved."

"All we can do now is decide to move on." Kiddo said. "It's hard, and it takes time, and I don't think we ever heal fully, but we move on and we learn to live again and love again and that makes us able to change the shapes of the holes in our hearts." Kiddo's eyes had filled with tears.

Blondie jutted her chin toward the doors Saundra usually used. Gold plaques had appeared above them.

One said move on, the other said don't move on. Black and white. Just as she liked.

"Go on," Blondie said. "See what's in store."

"But remember." Kiddo took her hand. "They are only possibilities."

Saundra stood and when she looked back, her two other selves were crawling back through the doors they'd come through. Their doors clicked shut.

Saundra's heart broke. She didn't want to do either of those things. She wanted Harvey. She wanted more time with him. And if she couldn't have that, she wanted to crawl into a hole and die.

She looked at Kiddo's door, then Blondie's. Harvey was still alive in their worlds or universes or whatever they were. She could go into one of them and find him, woo him like she'd done before, steal his heart, and have her happiness back.

She pulled Kiddo's door open and was confronted by a brick wall. She looked in Blondie's with the same result.

Saundra went back to her two doors, the options listed above them.

Move on or don't.

Black and white. Sort of.

But Saundra didn't have to go inside to see what would happen. She never had to come back to the room ever again if she didn't want to. Life wasn't meant to be controlled, even if the control was an illusion.

With a broken heart, she opened her eyes and left the room with all the doors. She sat in the hospital cafeteria with a cup of terrible coffee. The same place she sat before going into her mind.

She thought about what Kiddo said. About how the shapes of the holes in her heart could be changed. Maybe never filled in properly, but changed to accommodate a new life, a new love, new sorrow.

Saundra looked up toward the ceiling, toward the sky above outside. She vowed to Harvey that she would never stop loving him, but she would do her best to change the shape of the hole in her heart.

Ear Bleed

Margaret's husband was on the floor in the bathroom with blood coming out of his ear. His eyes were open, and he seemed alert and awake. She kneeled in front of him.

"Robert?" She gently shook his shoulder.

His eyes found hers, but he didn't speak.

"What's happening, Robert? What happened? Why are you bleeding? What's happening?" Her voice came out shrieky and hysterical. A voice he told her once he hated, because he knew when she used that voice, she was inconsolable and out of control. Beside herself with whatever emotion had taken her at the time, whether it be anger or fear or shock.

"Oh look, someone let the banshee out," he'd mutter, thinking she didn't hear him.

She'd heard him all right. She'd heard him loud and clear, every time he said it, including just that morning when she couldn't find her beloved cat, Spudski.

Robert's mouth opened and closed. Spittle dribbled from the corner of his lips. She smoothed his hair back and leaned in close to the ear that wasn't bleeding.

"Someone let the banshee out," she whispered. "Was your hearing aid turned up too high?" She leaned back and smiled kindly. "Did it burst your eardrum?"

Next time he would think twice before calling her a banshee.

Chrysalis

For Amanda

There was dirt everywhere, and no one knew why. The woman who lived there had been missing for several weeks. They'd only just gotten the forms signed to search her home.

It stank, too. Like the dirt had seen too much. Dirt from a deep dark place full of stagnant dead air. A place with rot and decay as the main event.

The team sifted through the dirt, looking for any reason for it, but found none. Not until they had it tested.

It wasn't dirt at all.

When they returned to the woman's house for further investigation—this time bringing along the city's most prominent entomologist—they found her body in the attic, withered and misshapen, split down the center. In the dark where her new form liked it.

After reviewing the results of the testing, the

entomologist informed the team to keep their flashlights off when they went in. They were to use night vision goggles and infrared.

Now, clustered around the opening to the ladder, one foolish team member—a guy who rarely followed orders, who'd been in trouble several times, and on administrative leave a handful, and who had been complaining about not being able to see properly ("my goggles are defective"), and all that—clicked on a flashlight.

The moment before the attack, they saw her true form in all its glory. The dusty fluttering wings, the frantic movements toward them, the strange, furry-looking protrusions coming out of the top of her head.

But in the end, it was her dead moth-eyes that left those who survived with broken minds.

Sunday afternoon was always the time to get stuff done. Last-minute stuff before the workweek began and ambition faded with early mornings and stress and the concept of "overworked, underpaid." Laundry, if not done on Saturday to get it out of the way, was done on Sunday during the game or before, depending on if there wasn't a lot and it was a late game.

This Sunday afternoon was different. Chores were left undone. The workweek didn't matter anymore. The buildings might not even be accessible anyway. Crowds of people, air raid sirens, soldiers in gas masks. No one went down there. They stayed inside unless they had the uniform and weaponry of the war.

It all happened fast, unexpected. But that's how war works, right? No one has "the war begins" written on their calendars, scheduled between a budget meeting and lunch with a potential new client. No one has a reminder sticker on Wednesday, crammed next to the birthday sticker for Auntie Hilda. It just happens. And that's what happened.

The laundry is still undone, heaps of it still covering

the flesh of the people who just one week ago would have washed those coveralls. Smoke fills the air. Dust, debris. The shouts of soldiers, an explosion, celebration by the enemy in an unknown tongue.

Heaps of laundry. It will never get done now. Not until the rains come and wash the blood from the street. Not until the sun comes back out and dries up all the rain.

Sunday afternoon. A time with family. Now it is a time lying dead atop a pile of laundry that isn't even yours.

Sunday afternoon. A dark time now. But, hey, at least the laundry doesn't have to be done.

Child Like Me

Genetic material can only be arranged in so many combinations before people start to look the same. As a result, science dictates everyone has at least seven Doppelgängers strewn around the world waiting to be found. Whether they are like the true Germanic folk-type, who will kill you and take over your life or not, who is to say?

I saw a child once who looked just like I did when I was a kid. He had the same scar down the side of his face and everything. It was from a stick-sword fight when I was five. We made eye contact at the park. He was eating a popsicle. I was running on the path around the lake. He seemed to be alone as there was no parent present. No nanny or grandmotherly type either. Just this kid, who looked like me, sitting on a bench watching me go by. I almost ran into someone else, his eye contact held me so solidly.

It wasn't the last I saw of him. In fact, I saw him more and more as the next week unfolded. I finally went to the library to do some research.

After pulling all the books I could on Doppelgängers

and look-alikes and all that—even pulled a few selections about clones—an old woman shuffled over to me.

"I couldn't help but notice the titles you've collected here," she whispered. Her voice held the hints of an Eastern European accent. "Is there a particular reason you are delving into this unusual subject?"

I snorted a laugh. How could I tell her what I'd seen? And yet, here I went.

"I saw a kid who looked like me when I was little," I said, absently thumbing the pages of the closest book. "It sounds crazy, but he seriously looked *just* like me. Like we could have been the same kid in different times. Or he could have been me from the past now in the present."

The woman nodded along. "This child ... he was alone, yes?" the woman asked.

"Yes," I said with too much enthusiasm, earning me a shush from a nearby patron. I whispered an apology and motioned for the woman to sit in the chair across the table from me. She sat.

"This is a rarity," she said. "Especially here in the states where there are so many people occupying so little space." She leaned forward. "But where I come from, it is not unusual to come across your *Kinterzvill*—your childlike twin."

If I hadn't seen this Kinterzvill myself, I would have thought she was crazy, even though I'd been a firm believer in Doppelgängers and ate up all the science fiction books and movies involving clones and look-alikes my entire life. To have something like this be ... real ... it was exciting.

"You won't find what you are looking for in these books." She patted the volumes on the table. "And you must be wary."

I gulped. I knew the German stories. It only made

sense that seeing this Kinterzvill would have some foreboding message behind it.

"Tell me," I whispered.

"One who makes contact of any kind with his own Kinterzvill will be hunted by it, and killed, unless he kills the Kinterzvill first."

I sat back. "Why? What does it want?"

"It wants to be the only one." She stabbed the table with an arthritic finger. "It recognizes the shared DNA. It feels threatened by it. By you. Like a male lion sensing another. It is driven by a primitive instinct we will never understand. It fights to kill."

"You said contact … like physical contact?"

"No." She shook her head. "The moment the Kinterzvill knows that you know about it, the hunt begins."

"I've seen him so many times this week," I said in a hollow voice. I swallowed hard, trying to get my throat to work properly. "Is there any other way?"

"I am afraid not," the old woman said, rising from her seat. "One must be ended. The Kinterzvill will stop at nothing." She leaned forward. "Good luck."

"Thank you," I said. "Thank you for telling me all of this."

She nodded gravely and shuffled off down the long rows of tables and out of the library. I wondered if she had been there waiting every day for some indeterminate amount of time—her entire life maybe—for some sad sap like me to come along to do the right research.

Now that she left, what she said sank in. It felt ridiculous in my head. A kid who just happens to look like me, hunting me down? Come on. Get real. I put the books on the re-shelving cart and left the library.

When I stepped out into the bright sunlight, I cringed and shielded my face.

Rapid footsteps sounded on the sidewalk. I looked around, but my eyes hadn't yet adjusted. Something hit my leg, and a sharp and burning pain erupted in my thigh. The footsteps dashed away. It was a kid.

I ran after the culprit. "Hey!" I yelled.

He looked over his shoulder. The scar. A jolt of electricity shot across my scalp. It was *the* kid. The Kinterzvill. I'm a runner, but the kid was fast. He easily outran me, giving me another chilly shock, and adding to the otherworldly intrigue the woman had built up around him.

"Hey buddy, you all right?" someone on the street asked. His eyes were on my leg.

I looked down. Through a tear in the fabric, a nasty gash spread blood like a blooming flower on my pants.

"I'm fine," I said. "Did you see a kid run this way?"

"Dude, you're bleeding. Are you sure you're okay?" the guy asked again.

I grabbed his arm. "Did you see a kid?"

The guy shook his head and wrenched his arm from my grip. He backed away before hurrying off.

The adrenaline left my system and the pain in my thigh burst to life. My knees shook. I leaned against the nearest building.

I limped home, and when I got there, locked the door and pulled the curtains shut.

"Okay," I said, breathless from rushing as quickly as I could to my safe haven. "Okay. Calm down. You don't know it was that kid." I knew it was that kid. "Dammit."

It was real.

I hobbled to the bathroom and pulled out all the first-aid crap I could find from under the sink. Gauze pads, wraps, bandages, suture strips, the whole nine yards. I patched my leg up as best I could, though it probably needed stitches. I could see some subcutaneous fat squishing out. But I didn't want to risk going outside again.

However, being inside meant the kid could hide somewhere outside my house and wait until I left. It gave him more time to prepare. It left me paranoid and sick with wasted adrenaline and anxiety.

A knock sounded at the door. I jumped, nearly screamed. A grown-ass man afraid of a little kid. I peered through the peephole but didn't see anyone. The kid would be too short to see through the peephole, if it were him. It probably was.

"Go away," I yelled. "Let's settle this another night."

Something scraped across the door. Probably the blade he'd slashed me with.

"Get out of here." I hit the door with my fist. A not-as-loud hit came from the other side.

I didn't own a gun, and I couldn't be one hundred percent sure it was him out there on the other side, but I was fairly certain it was. All I had was a knife collection my ex thought was ridiculous. Not so silly now, is it, babe?

In the guest room where I stored all my knives, I pulled a tactical knife from my collection and hooked it on my belt, then strapped on another military-grade blade around my good thigh. I had a sash full of ninja throwing stars. I pulled that on and cinched it tight. I finished my armament with a waistband sheath at the small of my back.

Glass shattered from the front of the house.

I scurried down the hall, back to the wall, and peeked around the corner into the front room. The curtain billowed inward with a gust of wind. Glass littered the ground beneath the window. A rock lay on the floor in the center of the room.

"Get out of here!" I yelled again. *Get off my lawn.*

"No." The little voice was inside the house. My heart skipped a few beats, and I sucked in a lungful of air to right the rhythm. I wasn't sure where the voice had come from, but it sounded like it was somewhere in the front of the house which included the dining room and kitchen.

I pulled a star from the sash across my chest and threw it against the opposing wall where it stuck in the plaster next to a picture of San Francisco that came with the frame.

The vase from the dining room table smashed into the room.

Location found. I gritted my teeth and dropped onto my stomach. I army crawled into the front room, separated by a half wall from the dining room.

The little bastard jumped onto my back and wrapped his arms around my neck. I stood and tried to shake him off, but he held tight. The glint of a steel blade in the corner of my eye told me he also had a tight grip on a sizeable knife—probably the chef knife from the block on the kitchen counter.

I grabbed his arms and bent over fast, shifting my shoulder to flip him over onto the floor. I pressed a boot into his belly. He squirmed and slashed at my leg with the kitchen knife, which I hadn't sharpened in a while. It was useless. I laughed and pressed harder on his little body. I didn't see that he had one of my throwing stars, pilfered during his initial attack, in his other hand. Not until he slammed it into the side of my calf.

I gripped my leg. The kid kicked me in the face. I fell backward.

· · ·

The fight went on for over an hour. He was relentless, resilient. A normal kid would have given up by now. But he was a lion, and I was a threat.

After the last round of ass-kicking, we lay across the room from each other, both bleeding, both battered, both with at least one throwing star stuck somewhere on our persons, maybe two.

The kid's arm lay at a strange angle next to him. We stared each other down. Extreme and unwavering eye contact.

"You can't win," I whispered. "I'm bigger and stronger than you." Yet, there I was, laying on the ground, bleeding and battered and maybe worse off than the kid.

He struggled to get up, like an overturned beetle.

I clutched my side and, with a groan and an explosive exhale, got up first. I shuffled over to him, barely able to lift either foot to walk. He flopped over onto his belly and got up that way. He turned around slowly, breath rasping in and out of his body. Blood from his nose trickled down his lip and around his mouth from both nostrils, giving him a Fu Manchu of blood.

"Give it up, kid," I said.

He stared, teeth clenched, shoulders heaving with angry breathing, for a few heartbeats. To my shock, he dropped his knife. His shoulders slumped. His little face— my face when I was a kid—contorted in sadness and pain and exhaustion. Wet sobs sniffled from his nose, followed by racking body shakes.

I didn't blame him. I was an adult and wanted to cry after all this.

"Truce?" I asked.

He seemed to consider the word and come to an agreement within himself. He lifted his arms out, one toward me, the other angled toward the ground, broken at the elbow, and raised his sad little red and tear-streaked face.

I bent a knee and opened my arms. The kid limped into my embrace. I wrapped my arms around his shuddering little body.

I didn't feel or hear the knife in the sheath at the small of my back slide out. But I felt his sobs turn to laughter right before he stabbed my own blade into my back. I felt it stab a little deeper when he shoved me onto my back.

The last thing I saw was his evil little face leering over mine. His little hand wiping away crocodile tears.

He doesn't know I survived his attack.

The last he knows, I died—a fake-out, of course. A last-ditch effort to survive. He didn't know to check for a pulse, maybe didn't know how, anyway. I heard him limp away, the front door open and slam shut.

It took a few surgeries to right the damage he did to me—broken ribs, internal bleeding, bruised kidneys, punctured lung—but I haven't seen him again. I carry a knife on me at all times now. I wear mirrored sunglasses. I watch and observe, looking for him, waiting to see him again.

Waiting to end the hunt.

Day Moon

"Beware the day moon."

A day moon? What the hell is a day moon?

Xavier Wallace walked outside into the late afternoon and looked up. A moon hung low in the sky, big and blue, across from the sun. How the hell did that get there? What did it mean? He thought the man at the brewery was bananas, but his words echo in Xavier's mind.

"Beware the day moon."

The beer churned in his stomach. Beware. Beware of what? Besides the day moon. What did it all mean?

Xavier turned down the sidewalk toward the blue, pocked ball in the sky. As he crossed the street, a car blasted its horn. He jumped back onto the curb.

He looked up at the moon. An anomaly in the bright sunshiny day.

Beware the day moon. Was that what the drunk at the brewery meant? Ill omens and shit? He looked both ways before crossing this time and carefully avoided a ladder propped against the concert hall where a woman changed out the letters of tonight's headliner.

Sweat beaded on his brow. The moon seemed bigger the next time he looked up. An oppressive force in the sky, pressing down on him, leering at him.

Beware … beware …

Noises on the street rose in volume, a mass of unsynchronized noise. He needed to get home, and fast.

Xavier sprinted, shoving by anyone who stood in his way. A businessman on his phone. A woman with a stroller and a screaming baby. His beard itched.

Beard?

He didn't have a beard. Xavier touched his chin. Yep. Beard. He turned to the storefront he stood in front of and looked at himself in the window. A strangled scream caught in his throat.

Staring back, his own reflection, was the crazy man from the brewery.

Box

Blood and slithery sliminess coated the box.

"What the actual hell is on the inside, if that's the outside?" Bill asked.

"Maybe the inside is dry. Like inside out boy from Pee-wee's Playhouse." Duke shrugged.

"That wasn't Pee-wee. It was some commercial on Nickelodeon. You're confusing him with Penny. They were both claymation."

Duke shook his head in disbelief and rolled his eyes. He looked at the box again. "Let's open it."

"No, man. No way." Bill held up his hands. He had a dream the other night. A dream he couldn't remember, but something about the box triggered his subconscious. A feeling of dread formed a cold stone in his gut.

The box shifted. They both jumped back.

A day ago, a moon hung over their small town in broad daylight. And now this. This horrible box. Another anomaly.

"Open it." Duke nudged Bill's shoulder.

Whispers of the dream Bill had forgotten filled him

with a terror so strong, he struggled to not pee his pants. He knew there was something terrible inside. Something neither of them wanted to see and would never forget. It would change them forever. Not in a good way, like finding a sack of cash. In a bad way, like finding a dead body in the woods. "Stand by Me" style. That movie gave him nightmares, and it wasn't even scary.

"You open it if you're so curious." Bill backed away, clenching and unclenching his fists.

Duke squatted in front of the box. The latch, if you could call it that, looked like fingers laced together. And maybe it was.

Duke pried the fingers apart. One broke off in his hand. He jumped back with a disgusted exclamation. The fingers slid apart with a sickening squishy slithering sound.

"I think we should leave it alone." Bill's voice barely left his lips.

Duke didn't crouch in front of the box this time. Now that it was unlatched, he used the toe of his boot to lift the lid. Bill squeezed his eyes shut and turned his face away.

Duke sucked in a gasp of air. The box slammed shut— Bill heard the fingers lace back together. When he opened his eyes, Duke lay on the ground unmoving.

Bill visited Duke in the long-term care facility once a week. He brought cards and dice to play their favorite games, though Duke hadn't said a word, nor expressed any sign of life ever since he saw whatever was inside that box.

Box of Hair

He shambled down the sidewalk with the box clutched against his ribs like a football. His matted hair lay plastered against his pate and forehead. Strips of dirty cloth wrapped his feet in makeshift shoes. The box puzzled all who noticed it gripped in his hand with fingernails long overdue for a trim.

Outside the bus, he shuffled by, quicker than most days, casting fear-filled glances over his shoulder. Three men stalked him, shouting and throwing their hands around. Anger painted the lines in their faces.

The man with the box tripped. The box flew from his grip. The lid popped off. A nest of hair—blonde, red, brown, black—tumbled out. Whose hair? Who knew?

The Smell

The smell permeated every inch of my nostrils, clinging to each nose hair and filling every pore. It was dirt, unwashed body, and greasy hair amalgamated with garbage and maybe excrement.

It came from a man clutching a box against his body. He was yards away, but the wind was right. Or wrong.

"Move it. You're ruining my day," I shouted.

The man turned, all herky-jerky movements, like his mind couldn't control the rest of him, and shuffled off. Me and my buddies followed him for a couple blocks, yelling at him until he tripped and fell. We took off before anyone could blame us.

Later that night, the smell came back. Maybe it hadn't fully left my nose, despite the nasal rinse. It got stronger and stronger. I opened my eyes just as he took out a knife and took a chunk of my scalp, opened the box, and placed it inside.

You Look Like an Emma

Harriet used to love her seasonal solo camping trips. They were a way to get away from it all. The hustle and bustle of the city, stresses of work, and other life's demands. She would pack up and drive into the mountains, pick a pull off, hike in, and make camp. No campground, no predetermined campsites, just Harriet and the wilderness.

On her last solo trip, she found a great place to pitch her tent. She removed any obvious rocks and set them to the side. She pulled out her tent, spread it out in the cleared spot, and went about setting it up. Satisfied with the placement, she unrolled her sleeping bag inside and stowed the rest of her gear. She used the rocks she'd removed from that spot, along with a few others nearby, and created a fire pit.

Harriet stood back and admired her campsite. Then she set off to collect firewood, which she stacked nearby. She piled some dry grass and small splintered sticks in the bottom of the firepit and made a teepee of larger sticks over it.

The snap of a twig brought her upright from her crouch.

A man in his late twenties jumped, his heavily laden pack almost throwing him backward. He grabbed a nearby tree for support.

"Oh, sorry," he said. "I didn't realize someone was up here."

"No worries," Harriet said. *Now move along.* She got to work striking her knife against a chunk of flint. Sparks jumped into the dry grass, igniting it.

"Do you mind if I pitch for the night?" He motioned to the sky. "Daylight's going. I don't think I can make it back in time."

Harriet did mind, but said, "Sure, go ahead. It's not my mountain."

He unslung his pack and started pulling gear out.

"In all my time coming here," he said. "I've never crossed paths with anyone."

"Yep," Harriet muttered. She was not in a chatty mood. She could see the guy grinning out of the corner of her eye, like he'd never seen another person before.

"Look." She paused, arranging kindling around the small fire. "I don't mean to be rude or whatever, but I come up here a few times a year to get away from people. I'm not really up for small talk."

He nodded. "I get it, I get it." He set up his camp in silence, aside from the occasional confused whispers when he pitched his tent, and again when he couldn't light a fire.

He came over to the edge of her fire's light. "Uh," he said with a nervous laugh. "Do you mind, uh, sharing your fire?"

Harriet stifled a groan.

"All I brought is soup." He motioned to his dead fire pit. "Can't get a spark to save my life."

"Fine," Harriet said.

He dragged a camp chair over, clattering it across the grass and dirt and rocks instead of folding it and carrying it like a civilized human being. He sat down and cracked the lid on his pull-top soup can, then set it down low in the pit.

"I'm Donald, by the way."

Harriet gave him her best do-not-disturb look and sighed. It was one night.

"Harriet," she said.

"You look more like an Emma." He chuckled and shook his head. "Sorry. Force of habit."

"From what?"

"I used to work security at a bank," he said as if that explained it. "I used to guess peoples' names based on their looks and how they dressed." He laughed through his nose.

"How often were you right?" Harriet asked.

He shrugged. "I never knew their names."

They were quiet for a few moments and he laughed again.

"Great story, Donald. Stupid."

Harriet laughed, despite herself.

"It's fine," she said. "What makes me look like an Emma?"

"Big, wide eyes. Like almond-shaped, not wide open," he said. "Like Emma Stone." He shook his head. "It's so dumb."

Harriet snorted a laugh through her nose.

"If we were all normal, the world would be a boring place," she said. "And yes, I am implying that you aren't normal."

He barked a laugh at that. "Pretty *and* funny. I like that, though. The boring place thing." He pulled his soup can out of the fire with a pair of pliers.

They chatted a bit longer. Donald told Harriet his life story while she casually interjected at times but didn't tell him a thing about herself. She turned in while the fire was still going strong. Donald said he would stay up and monitor it.

He left before she got up the next morning. She stretched and smiled.

"Peace and quiet," she whispered. She spent three days and three nights hiking around the mountain, snapping pictures of birds, flowers, critters, deer, anything that caught her eye. She didn't see a single other person and returned to civilization rested and re-energized to tackle whatever life brought her way. Ready to take on the hardest of challenges.

When she got home and downloaded the pictures from her camera, however, icy chills clawed up her spine, chasing away the meditative warmth of a mental vacation.

Interspersed among the daily hiking photos she'd taken—the birds, deer, critters, flora, and such—were pictures of herself. Sleeping.

The Wind

I feel the wind on my arm and leg. Left and right respectively. It moves the hairs, ruffles them. I always thought it strange when the hair grew long enough to feel the wind in it. I haven't shaved that leg in months.

A gust flutters the hairs again. It tickles. I reach to scratch my arm, to rub away the gooseflesh that has arisen there. My hand hits nothing. I look down. Down where my arm should be, where my hand touched nothing but air, and then my ribcage.

There is nothing there. For the briefest of moments, I believe my arm has become invisible. Invisible in sight and matter.

I keep forgetting. I lost my arm and leg in a car accident last month.

You Open the Door

A Choose Your Own Adventure With No Choices

The last thing you remember is putting on your shoes to meet some friends at a new escape room venue called Escape Room 237 for your birthday. The new venue promised to blend the thrill of a Halloween haunted house attraction with the joy of solving an escape room! You were excited. Two things you love blended together? Yes, please!

You awaken on the bare hardwood of an unfamiliar room. Small doors—large cupboards, really—line the walls. Four on each side. In the center is a table covered with dissimilar and unconnected items. You get up to check it out and find: a potted flower, an envelope opener, a box of crayons, a piece of wood, a hammer and nails, a slingshot with what looks like a silver brooch, a bag of sunflower seeds, and a gas torch.

Behind you is a larger door. You try the knob, but it is locked. There is a folded note taped to it with your name scrawled on it. You pull it down and unfold it.

Welcome to Escape Room 237. In order to win, you must survive The Room With All the Doors. Failure to survive will result in death.

There is no signature at the bottom. Just a friendly smiley face.

You smirk and don't take the note seriously. It's just a game, after all. Right?

You wander the room and look at each door. The first is closed with a latch. The next has a red stain—maybe ketchup—on it. The third door has a child's drawing taped to it. The next one is unpainted. The natural wood is knotty pine. The fifth has a moon painted on it. Door number six has feathers sticking out of the crack. The seventh, a hole in the middle. A cursory peek inside shows nothing but darkness. And finally, the last door has a framed pressed flower hanging on it.

THE LATCH

You start with the door with the latch on it, not because you like to live dangerously, but because you don't even stop to think the latch might be keeping something inside. You flick the latch and the door creaks open three inches. Inside lies unfathomable darkness. You immediately shut the door and back away, but since you failed to latch it, it falls open again. You hear a haunting wail from inside.

"Hello?" you shout from the safety of five feet away. "Is someone in there? I've unlocked it. You can come out."

You realize—a little late, don't you think?—that maybe whatever is wailing in there isn't supposed to come out.

It's just a game.

A putrid white and gnarled hand grips the door frame in that dank blackness. A foot slides out across the floor, leaving a trail of slime and blood behind it. The thing that emerges from the dark cupboard double-jointedly crawls across the floor toward you, wailing with a mouth too large and too black for its face, curtained by black stringy matted hair. You back away and circle around to the table of seemingly random items. You grab the flowerpot and chuck it at the beastly banshee. The pot breaks in front of her, spilling the soil and flower onto the wooden floor. She halts.

In a series of grinding, crackling twists, she unwinds herself from her double-jointed pose and picks up the flower.

"Violet," she says in a harsh whisper. She races back to the cupboard with the latch, flower clutched against her chest. She turns at the doorway and gives you a gruesome grin. "I'll see you later." She climbs inside, and you rush to slam it and latch it behind her.

The haunted house attraction element on the first go. And great acting to boot.

You rub your hands together, let out a nervous laugh, and look at the other doors. Seven to go.

THE HANDPRINT

A knock comes from beyond the next door, the one with what looks like a ketchup stain on the outside, as if someone ate french fries or hot wings and didn't wash their hands before coming up to the room.

"Hello? Who is it?" you call at the door in a sing-song voice. The knocking comes again.

You open the door. A hand flies out of the darkness toward you. It latches onto your face like the face-grabbing alien in that sci-fi film you watched when you were too young to watch it.

You fall backward, feet kicking, scrabbling for purchase

while the hand's fingernails dig into the skin around your eyes and cheeks. The pinky works its way into your eye, gouging. You cry out, and the thumb hooks inside your cheek. You bite down hard, grinding your front teeth back and forth. The taste of blood fills your mouth, and the hand somehow screams a pained shriek. It leaps away, hissing, and scuttles around the floor, back and forth like an angry crab.

Every time you try to move, it lunges forward, long yellow nails scratching at the floor, gouging lines into the layers of varnish.

You reach up, blindly groping the tabletop for something to throw. Your hand grips the first thing it touches. The box of crayons. Likely ineffective, but you shrug and chuck them at the thing. The box of crayons explodes, sending waxy coloring sticks across the floor. The hand seems distracted. You reach again and get the envelope opener.

While the hand has its … back … turned, you attack, but it turns and leaps for your face again. You lift the envelope opener to block the attack and lunge forward, pinning the hand to the blood-stained cupboard door.

It shrieks and writhes. You unpin it while keeping it kabobbed on the mail opening tool, open the door, and toss it inside, dull blade and all.

You slam the door and lean against it, heart pounding so fast you might have a heart attack at any moment. You get your breath back. A small part of you is beginning to suspect this isn't just a game.

THE DRAWING

You back away from the door with the handprint—you

now know it *is* a bloody handprint, as you've added more of the same to it. The next door has the crayon drawing of a faceless stick figure in a top hat.

You turn the knob, unlatching the door, and back away without fully opening it.

A black hand with long fingers reaches out and uses the door and the frame to pull itself out of the dark beyond. It unfolds itself to reveal a man without a face. He is tall and lanky and wears all black. Just like the crayon rendition of him on the door. In fact, his edges are even a little grungy and smeary.

"Oh for Pete's sake," you mutter.

The figure lurches upright. The head cocks to the side and you realize, somehow, even without ears, the thing heard you.

The figure advances, groping blindly. You sidestep and scan the table, but none of the tools left there seem to make sense.

The thing circles around, seeming to home in on your ragged breathing. Your foot slips on something, and you nearly go down, but catch yourself. A crayon rolls across the floor. The rest of them are behind the figure. You rush around the table, but it hears you and circles back. You dive under the table just as the thing lunges, arms swiping to grab you. You skid to a stop and grab the first crayon to hit your sweaty palm and rush to the door.

Unsure if this is the right move, you finish the drawing by adding two eyes to the face with the blue crayon you grabbed from the floor. You look up just in time to ninja roll out of the way of the man stalking after you. He swipes out, dragging a claw across your shoulder. Pain blooms as three jagged gashes leak blood down your arm. You run to the opposite side of the room.

He now has eyes. The better to see you with, my dear.

"I'm trying to help you," you shout. The eyes merely blink. He's now blocking the door and the unfinished drawing. Perhaps a smiley face will make him more … amicable.

You dodge left. He follows. You dodge right. Same. You slide under the table and between his legs and swipe your hand out toward the drawing. Your attempt at a mouth is a jagged downward slash on the lower part of the head. You roll away again.

The face looks angry. The mouth opens and closes. Inside are sharp gnashing teeth. The now angry stickman stomps his feet and shakes his fists. If he hadn't shredded your shoulder, the whole thing might be comical.

As you circle around the table again, you step on something that flings your leg out in front of you. You land hard on your back, wrenching your torn shoulder. Blood splatters the floor. The figure stomps around the table, lifting its knees high, as if wanting to smash your head with his—you just now realize—footless leg.

It was another damn crayon you slipped on. You roll away before the drawing-come-to-life can get you.

Back at the door, you snatch the drawing off the door and crumple it into a ball. The figure twists and distorts along with it. You twist the paper. A pained scream comes from the distorted live crayon lines. A pathetic sound. A sound that says you win. You use the gas torch from the table to burn it.

A triumphant and slightly hysterical laugh exits through your clenched teeth as you watch the crayon man distort along with the smoldering paper.

You move to replace the torch on the table among the sunflower seeds, slingshot, and hammer with nails, but decide to keep it. This is definitely not a game, and these are definitely not actors.

. . .

GOT STRINGS?

The unpainted door catches your eye. The knots no longer seem naturally placed. As you look at them, they blink. You step back, uncertain, and scan the items on the table, and in the seconds of distraction, a loud crack issues from the door.

The wood panels splinter. You watch in horror as the wood warps and shifts and things emerge. At first, you aren't sure what they are, but they step out of the woodwork, dragging strings behind them like umbilical cords connected to the door. They detach with a tearing sound.

Marionettes.

They all have faces formed by the lines of the natural wood they are made of. Three of them to start with, and more come out as you watch. They congregate by the door, staring at you.

They lurch toward you, strings dragging behind them. One of them even drags a leg, and you wonder if they are tiny zombies, which makes you subsequently wonder if they will try to eat your brains. There doesn't appear to be anything on the table that could stop them, but the torch in your hand might do some damage. Too bad there isn't a can of gasoline. You press the igniter, and the flame leaps from the tip.

The marionettes pause.

The flame vanishes. You click the igniter over and over to no avail. It's out of gas. You used it on the wrong obstacle. You toss the torch to the side and prepare to take on the tiny wooden people.

They stalk toward you at a slow pace. This should be

easy. You can outrun them for days. Probably get around behind and grab them all up and shove them back into—

You realize their door never opened. They came *out* of it, not through it. Or maybe through it, but in a spirit kind of way.

The wooden people keep following, now rasping with brittle rattling voices. *Rasp rattle groan.*

As you pass by the door with the moon painted on it, you hear scratching and growling. A sharp bark and a yip followed by more scratching.

A dog?

Dogs like sticks. The marionettes are basically little people made of sticks. As you circle back, something snags your foot and you fall flat onto your belly. A marionette used its own string as a lasso. The string tightens around your ankle, cutting into your leg through your pants. You roll onto your back just as another loop flings toward you. You bat it away. It somehow snags your index finger and tightens painfully. The tip of your finger turns an angry reddish-purple.

The door with the moon rattles in its frame.

A dog would be salvation and a welcome companion. You try to stand, but the little man yanks on the string, pulling your leg straight. Another lasso snags the end of your shoe and pulls your other leg out. Trying to kick your legs is useless. These little wooden monsters have the strength of ten men.

You try to crawl backward on your elbows, but the one guy has your finger in a vice-like grip. He jerks the string and now your arm is pulled straight out, forcing you to bend forward at the waist painfully.

You whistle toward the door with the moon.

"Come here, dog," you shout, your voice wavering with fear and adrenaline.

Thumping ensues from the other side, but the door holds. The marionettes choke up on the strings, looping them as they go. If you could get some purchase—

You slide your butt forward, which allows your knees to bend, and slack to form in all three strings. You use the slack to jerk your arm backward. The marionette attached to your finger flies onto his face. With the slack at your ankle and foot, you get to your feet and try to run. They pull back with all their might, but not before you've made it a short distance around the table, pulling them behind you. They pull back hard and yank your feet out from under you, inches from the door with the dog behind it.

You reach up, but it's the hand with the string tied to your finger, which is now a sick dark purple color. The marionette pulls the string, wrenching your arm backward painfully.

Your other arm is free. You reach for the door handle, but it is still inches away. You swing your arm back and try again. Closer. Again. Closer still. Finally, you fling one more time, ignoring the pain that has started in your calves, and latch onto the handle. It pulls down. The door opens.

A fury of gray fur explodes out of the darkness and leaps over you. You hear growling and screaming and the clatter of wood. When you look back, it's a giant timber wolf shaking the marionettes to pieces.

One of the wooden people drags itself toward you with its remaining arm. Another sits groping the area where its legs should be, the lines on its face confused and horrified at once.

The rest are in similar states of mangle. Wood fragments litter the floor.

While the wolf destroys the tiny wooden people, you

take stock. Miniscule bloody bite marks mar your pant legs. Those little bastards!

The cries stop. The sound of splitting wood ceases. You look up and make eye contact with the wolf.

HOWLER

The wolf stares at you. Its eyes are yellow and predatory. It issues a low growl, then throws its head back and howls. The howl becomes a pained roar. The wolf's body cracks and shifts, as if something inside is trying to burst out through its skin. And burst through it does. Skin fragments fly in every direction, pelting you with … well … pelt … and blood and sinew.

The slingshot and brooch enter your mind, and you snag them from the table as the wolf shifts from feral beast to half man.

Before it can get too comfy in its new form, you pull back on the slingshot's cup and rubber tubes and let loose with the silver brooch.

It hits the wolfman square between the eyes. He lets out a pained *yipe* but doesn't seem otherwise phased.

Your only hope is to retrieve the brooch and try again. The wolfman, now enraged by the injury you inflicted—minor as it was—leaps onto the table, almost toppling it with his weight, and snarls at you as you back away and sidle around.

You thrust the slingshot at it as if it were a sword. The wolfman leaps back once but is undeterred by the second stabbing motion. You dive for the brooch at the same time the wolfman leaps at you. It snaps your calf in its jaws, just as your fingers snatch the silver jewelry.

You load the cup while the wolfman chomps happily

on your leg. The pain doesn't register, there's so much adrenaline pumping through your system.

Once again, you pull back on the cup and let loose the brooch. This time, the brooch embeds itself in his eye.

The wolfman screeches and paws at his face. The silver mixes with his blood, or something like that. Smoke rises from the eye socket. The screeches become howls. Canine-like cries. It's horrible to hear. Covering your ears does nothing against the sound.

The smoke turns into embers that race across the beast's head. It keeps pawing at the burning fur and flesh. In a matter of seconds, the room fills with the scent of singed hair and burned meat. The wolfman thrashes around, letting out low howls and wails.

You almost feel sorry for it. Almost.

But then the pain in your calf registers. You realize most of your muscle—and favorite pants—is missing.

The smoldering carcass turns to ash while you fight back tears and cries of agony. You tear off the sleeve of your shirt and tie it around your calf, completely unaware that another door has opened.

THE FLOCK

A chicken comes out of the darkness. Just one, clucking and pecking at any tiny thing it can find on the floor. It struts around in jerky movements, cocking its head in every direction as if taking in the room. You let out a sigh of relief. One chicken. Not too bad. You can handle a chicken.

You lean your head back against the wall and close your eyes, taking deep breaths. When you open them, the chicken is standing between your legs down by your feet.

Its beak is pointed straight at you, so you know it isn't looking at you, per se, but it *is* eerie.

The ruffle of feathers draws your attention beyond this immediate chicken, where a full flock, at least fifty brown bodies, fill the room. The scent of dusty bird feathers and guano immediately permeates the air.

There is a rustle through the flock as they make soft chicken noises. The one by your feet pecks at your shoelace. Another chicken struts over, followed by another.

Flock mentality has them all fighting for your shoelace in a matter of moments, and then they peck at the bloody flesh peeking out from under your makeshift bandage.

You kick your leg. They scatter, flapping their useless wings, but in a second, they are on you again, standing now, with their weighty bodies on your legs as if your lower appendages are roosting racks for their slumber. The weight of their bodies presses against your knees.

What's a henway?

The old joke goes through your head, and you respond to yourself.

"About three to five pounds."

These hens weigh far more than that, based on the crush of them. You shake them off again and try to get to your feet, but now they rush at you, flapping their wings and attacking with their clawed feet. You cry out as one slams you in the gut and another scratches your cheek while you're doubled over.

They cluster around you so tightly, you can hardly lift your feet to move through them. They violently peck at any parts of you they can reach. You slog through the feathery bodies, swinging your arms and legs as best you can while their assaults continue. When you reach the table, you grab the bag of sunflower seeds at the same time a massive rooster leaps onto the table for the same thing.

His viciously clawed foot lands on top of your hand and digs in. You make extreme eye contact for a few long seconds before he jabs at your face with his beak, catching you in the eye. You grab your face and lean away too far. The bodies of this rooster's concubines seem to grip your legs. You fall back, windmilling your arms to fix your balance, and grab the rooster by the neck as you go. His feet kick the trunk of your body as you fall, tearing at your shirt and skin. You land on top of several chickens who failed to get out of the way. You feel bones crunch under your torso and hope it was theirs and not your own.

The rooster continues his assault, wings flapping. You keep your hold on his scrawny neck. The hens have regained confidence after your fall and are moving closer again with their jerky clucking movements.

The rooster wrenches in your grip and breaks his own neck. You fling the lifeless bird aside. The hens leap on it, pecking until blood speckles the white walls around them.

While they are otherwise preoccupied, you crawl over to the table, dragging your bloody calf behind, and grab the bag of sunflower seeds.

"Here chicky chicky," you call in a weak and crumbling voice. You thrust your hand into the bag and toss a fistful of seeds toward the nearest chickens, then another trailing toward their open door. When most of them have their attention on you, you chuck handfuls into the open door until all of them disappear inside. You launch your battered and bloody body at the door and close them all inside.

THE HOLE

You crawl away and look at the next door. The door with the hole in it.

A black spiny thing pokes out of the gaping hole and twitches around. It is about the size of a stick you would use to play fetch with a dog, but hairy and feeling around for something. Probably you.

"Oh, hell no," you groan. You grab the board, hammer, and nails and slap the board over the hole. The oversized insect-like appendage flops around, trying to pull back in but unable. As you hammer the nails in, it touches your face, shoulders, arms. You relent and shift the board. The feeler sucks back inside. You finish the job, covering the hole completely.

VIOLET

One door remains. The one with the pressed flower hanging on it from a tiny hook. You slide to the floor in front of the door with the now-covered hole in it, gasping for air, blood leaking from various parts of your body, vision blurred, eyes watering.

The door doesn't appear to have a knob on the outside, but it has the hardware to suggest there is one on the inside.

You will it to stay shut, but, having been through all of this already, you know it won't. As you lay there, you cry. Hot tears trickle down your cheeks, burning in all the places where the chickens and the rooster pecked and mutilated you. Your eyes both hurt, and you thank whatever holy thing might be out there that you can still see.

The door creaks open and a beautiful face appears around the edge. Bright blue eyes, a stark contrast to the fair skin and black hair. She seems familiar.

She looks at you, then across the room to the door with the latch. Door number one.

"No," you whisper, face contorting. "Don't." Now you know. The girl-thing from the first door. This girl looks like her, before she got all gross and stuff.

The pretty girl steps out from behind the door, leaving it open. She wears a white lacy knee-length dress and no shoes. She side steps toward the other door.

"No," you plead, reaching a hand toward her. You are too tired to move to stop her. Besides, you can't feel the leg with the torn calf anymore, let alone move it.

She giggles and takes another step, then another. She raises her arm straight out from her side, eyes locked on yours the entire time. Her finger flicks the latch.

The door opens.

The double-jointed creature girl emerges.

"Violet," she says in a pleased voice. She hands the flower to the pretty girl. They embrace. They dance as if it has been millennia since they've seen each other. It's all very cute and sweet yet terrifying because they both stop at the same time and turn to look at you as if you are at the end of a creepy hallway in a haunted hotel.

They stalk toward you. The pretty girl jerks and cracks. Eyes of all sizes appear across her forehead. All round and black and shining. Her arms grow coarse black hair, and to your utter horror, more of them shoot out of her body as she drops to her hands and knees, only now they aren't hands and knees, but the blunt ends of spider legs.

She scuttles toward you.

The grody girl-thing is at the spider's side and gives it a pat on the head.

"I told you I'd see you again," she says in that horrible rasping voice. "It's been so long since Violet has had a snack."

In a movement too quick for your injured eyes and

sensibilities to comprehend, the spider bites your neck. You grow numb and heavy. Your head sags to the side.

The spider lifts you against its body with two of its legs and carries you through the door into the darkness.

You don't feel a thing as she gently wraps you in silk. You are completely unaware when the silk covering your face cuts off your air supply.

Thank goodness for tranquilizing venom.

****YOU HAVE FAILED TO ESCAPE THE ROOM WITH ALL THE DOORS****

Her Eyes

Her eyes, her smile, her beautiful hair. Her hand in my hand, her eyes meet mine. Cold nights, quiet mornings. Pillow talk, coffee talk, silences between. Early days of lust turning to the comfort of love becomes the necessity of companionship. Lives merge. Two to one. Duplicate items are cast aside. Never alone. Always together. You and me. Days, months, years. Together but never together.

Jokes once funny fail to bring a smile. Habits once thought cute or quirky are annoying. The necessary companionship withers to willful tolerance, breaks down to hardly contained irritability. Smiles become scowls become shouts to take out the goddamned trash. Words of affection become phrases of anger. Always and never. A heated moment—not by passion, by hate—goes too far.

Her lifeless eyes, her non-existent smile, her blood-crusted yet beautiful hair.

I will miss the warmth of her body the most.

For Wissa

The skin tag in my armpit had grown to a size I was no longer comfortable with. It grossed me out, so I can't imagine how others felt about it when they saw it dangling there like a tiny testicle.

It was around the size of a pencil eraser, held on by a tiny string of skin. Easy enough to handle removal at home with a pair of sanitized cuticle scissors. When it was done, I accidentally dropped the removed ball of skin and couldn't find it anywhere.

"I'll get it the next time I vacuum." I waved the lost remnant of my body away and went about my day.

A month's worth of vacuuming went by. I'd forgotten about the skin tag. It was spring now and raining outside. A constant drizzle. The perfect day to tackle cleaning out closets and maybe even the garage.

I opened the hall closet—the one that, in a cartoon,

would spill all assortment of things onto the floor. Coats, old sporting equipment, abandoned toys the kids no longer played with but couldn't bear to part with yet.

I heard a hiss, not unlike a cat. Then a small and helpless whimper.

A cold prickle tingled across my scalp and coursed down my back.

In the corner sat a lumpy little thing. At first, I thought it was a deflated football. It was a light brownish pink color, fleshy in all areas. It had a round belly and a misshapen head. Tiny appendages hung like vestigial limbs from its torso. Its face sloped across its little head. Wide eyes held in with fleshy flaps. No nose. A mouth that was just a gash in its face.

It reached its arms toward me.

"Ma … mama …" The voice was thick and phlegmy.

I closed the door, only then remembering the lost skin tag. This thing was the same color. The same texture. It looked like a larger version of it. It was a piece of me. A removed part clipped away and abandoned.

I opened the door again.

The pathetic little thing, slumped there in the corner, looked up at me. It flopped onto its side and, using its thin and weak little arms, dragged itself toward me. It placed a tiny three-fingered hand on my foot before dropping its face against the floor.

Wet breathing sounds gurgled against the hardwood. I bent and rolled it over gently. It was warm and squishy. I lifted it into my arms.

It blinked at me. Two slow blinks. The gash of a mouth opened in what I could only describe as a smile.

"Let's get you something to eat," I said. "My little pet."

Mine

Festering blood sores cover your body, leaking illness and disease. I can heal you. It is my talent, my gift. I make things. I take things apart and put them together. Sewing seams that would not make sense in the natural world. Piecing together the masks and facades of lives no longer among the living.

These creatures are healed beings freed from pain. Creatures who lie dormant and waiting. Empty shells, empty eyes, putrid souls escaped. They are my children. I cared for them. I freed them.

You can be like them. You will be like them. I see the light fading in your face. The blood sores weep like the sadness in your eyes.

Soon I will awaken them. Soon they shall stalk the earth in freedom. I shall set them free once again, but not from the pain this time, but to live anew with the life I have breathed into them. The life I have raised within them.

Until then, they belong to me. They are mine. Just as you belong to me. Just as you are mine.

Life After Life

Roger Alaster refused to heed the warnings of the locals. He wanted to get his new boutique hotel—the kind that was more like a bed and breakfast—up and running by the start of the summer.

He'd inherited the land by some turn of luck. The records showed his great-great-grandfather—Montgomery Alaster, a man with whom Roger shared a remarkable resemblance—had some percentage of ownership. Roger was the only descendant that the powers that be could identify and locate.

Despite his heritage, Roger knew he wasn't welcome in the small mountain town—yet. He didn't let that stop him from having a positive attitude and friendly nature toward them, though. More flies with honey, and all that.

"Ain't no hotel last more 'n' a year or two on that plotta land," the local hardware store manager told him as he dropped Roger's change into his hand. "Land's cursed."

It wasn't the first time that guy had told him that, and it wouldn't be the last. He said it every time Roger set foot in his store.

He heard it from everyone. Sometimes directly to his face, sometimes in whispers around the local diner.

"City shoulda bought it up."

Roger heard a couple speaking in low tones at the Squatting Frog—the town's only restaurant, and a greasy spoon at that. "Shoulda bought it up and not allowed no one to build on it. Shoulda condemned it." The man, Clancy, whom Roger had met at some weekly town event, kept on, his voice rising in volume.

Roger could see Leeta, Clancy's wife, casting furtive glances Roger's way in the mirror behind the counter where he sat on a swiveling stool.

"Keep your voice down, Clancy," Leeta said. "He's right there."

"I don't care. He needsta know." His face was an angry red. His lower lip trembled.

Roger turned to the couple and rose off the barstool.

"Oh, I know all right. Don't you worry." He wiped his mouth on his napkin, fished a twenty out of his wallet, and went to the door.

"Got-damn city just wants to make money off these no good outta towers," Clancy said. Leeta shushed him with a placating hand on his wrist.

"You have a good day now," Roger said with a smile.

He'd been in Fairhaven for the better part of a year. Permits took time, after all. They'd broken ground a few months ago and had about a month left on the build. Progress was moving along quickly, which pleased Roger. The sooner the hotel opened, the sooner the townsfolk would see it wasn't going to hurt anyone.

When he arrived at the site, a woman sat on the front porch. She wore strange attire. Old-timey. Long skirt, high-collared blouse with puffy sleeves.

She wasn't wearing a hard hat.

When she lifted her gaze to Roger's, he found she was mystifyingly beautiful, with auburn hair and blue eyes.

Those eyes widened in what seemed like surprise. "Monty?"

"Roger," he said. "Roger Alaster. You can't be on the site without a hard hat."

She rose to her feet and moved outside of the chain-link fence.

"What can I do for you?" Roger expected another litany of warnings. He'd never seen her around town, and he was sure he knew everyone by face if not by name. But something about her seemed familiar. Something way down deep in the recesses of his mind. Maybe he'd seen a picture of her somewhere.

To his surprise, she smiled demurely and lowered her eyes coquettishly in a way lost to the digital age.

"I just wanted to tell you how pleased I am that you are rebuilding the hotel," she said. Her voice was soft and the epitome of feminine. Roger had only heard voices like hers on period shows or movies set in the Victorian age. Her clothing seemed to match the latter.

Roger smiled and adjusted his hard hat. "Thank you," he said. "You seem to be the only one, Miss ..." He held his hand out to her.

"Gloria," she said. "Gloria Firestone, of the Fairhaven Firestones?" She tucked her fingers into his hand as if expecting him to kiss her knuckles. He resisted the urge. Chivalry was another art lost to the digital age, and to the #metoo movement.

"I best leave you to your work, Mr. Alaster." She pulled on a pair of wrist-length gloves and walked up the sidewalk, head up toward the late spring sun.

Roger watched her go, bewildered by the brief encounter.

. . .

He saw her a lot during the last weeks of construction. She would walk by or appear almost out of nowhere to say hello and inquire about the progress of the hotel. He wondered if she worked for some tourist attraction he somehow wasn't aware of, because she always wore her period costume. Whenever they spoke, he forgot to ask.

The Fairhaven Suites Boutique Hotel opened only a week over schedule on a stormy afternoon. Roger styled it after an old saloon to fit into the rustic qualities of the town. It had a covered front porch that spanned the width of the building, with rocking chairs on one side and a porch swing on the other.

He held a grand opening event. Gloria attended, and he grinned at her beaming at him from the crowd while everyone else wore sullen and grouchy faces.

"I know none of you are happy about this," he said, spotting even Clancy and the hardware store owner among the faces. "But thank you for coming out anyway."

The mayor begrudgingly stepped onto the wide front porch and said a few words.

"We've needed a hotel for a while." He gave a curt nod and cut the ribbon.

Roger had a spread of snacks on a table in the hotel's dining room and all ten rooms open for people to tour.

He noticed a few people smiling and nodding in what appeared to be approval. At the end of the event, as people filtered out, he heard someone say, "It's just like that old hotel. Just like it. A replica."

"Excuse me, sir," Roger called to the man. The old man, who Roger recognized as Old Bill Shay, clung to another man's arm, Billy Jr., his grandson. "Can you tell me what happened to the old hotel?"

The man looked like he was old enough to be Billy Jr.'s *great*-grandad.

"Owner set fire to it! Nobody knows why. But burn it did! To the ground! Nothing left!" He released his grandson's arm and took a wobbly step toward Roger. "Everyone inside perished, including most of the Fairhaven Firestones."

"Grandpa." Billy Jr. reached for his grandfather, but Old Bill Shay waved him off.

"Fairhaven Firestones?" Roger asked.

"Rich family moved to town, bought out the hotel to live in. Had some deal with the owner. They cursed the land and the town. Bought the mountain and mined it. Released some evil, or maybe Mother Nature or God got mad. Who knows? Everything they and their descendants touched turned to shit." Spittle flew from his quivering lips.

"Grandpa." Billy Jr. reached again and seized his grandfather's arm. Old Bill Shay allowed it.

"Land's cursed. I told you that when I first saw you."

"I know," Roger said.

"Turned 'em evil!" Old Bill Shay shouted as his grandson gently ushered him out. They were the last to leave.

Thunder rumbled in the ominous clouds collecting overhead.

Roger laughed through his nose and returned to the dining room to clean up the food. He piled it in the kitchen by the big sinks. While he cleaned, he thought about marketing strategies to reel in business. Based on what he'd learned from Old Bill Shay, he even considered calling the place a haunted hotel to attract business from out-of-towners.

"The Haunted Fairhaven Hotel," he muttered. "Site of the Firestone Family Massacre." He chuckled and scraped the last dish into the trash. "Most haunted hotel in all of Colorado."

"Mr. Alaster," a voice said.

Roger shrieked. He dropped the dish. It broke at the bottom of the trashcan. He whirled around. Gloria stood in the doorway with a fine fingered hand over her mouth. Her eyes seemed to laugh.

"You scared the hell out of me," Roger said. "I thought everyone left."

She giggled. "I was upstairs, waiting for them all to go." She came closer. "It's just beautiful." She motioned above her head, indicating the rooms on the second floor, he imagined.

Roger grinned.

"Everything is just perfect." She clasped her hands in front of her.

"I'm glad you like it." He returned to the sink and filled it with soapy water. "What do you know about what happened to the Fairhaven Firestones?" Roger asked boldly.

Gloria's smile faded. Her eyes grew glassy and distant. The lights flickered and, in their strobe-like effect, her face changed from pensive to sinister with a too-wide grin and darkness around her eyes as if they were sunken and black instead of blue. It lasted for the briefest second, and then her beautiful face returned.

Roger wasn't even sure if he'd seen it right, but he knew he had. His shaking hands when he lifted the soapy sponge to wash a platter told him. He focused on washing the platters, aware Gloria was still in the doorway watching him. From the corner of his eye, she leaned against the doorjamb.

"My family were unliked," she said, gazing at nothing. "The town folk here don't like strangers."

Roger gave a mirthless snort. "You can say that again."

"It was different. Back then it was open hatred." She smoothed her hand over her skirt. "They accused us of bringing evil here. Can you believe that?" Her eyes met his.

Based on what Old Bill Shay had said, Roger could believe it. If he believed it was true was another story. He gave Gloria an indifferent and tiny shrug. When she didn't continue, Roger turned to her and dried his hands on a towel.

"Your family mined the mountain?" he asked.

Gloria nodded. "We bought it fairly first, of course," she said. "The townsfolk … they warned us not to mess with it. They told us we were asking for trouble. The only one who accepted us was the owner of the hotel. He let us buy out the rooms to live here until we finished our work, or until we built our own house."

The way she spoke made it sound like she had been there.

"Your family, you mean?" Roger asked, needing to hear her say she wasn't there, especially after that flickering change to her face.

"I beg your pardon?"

"I mean, you weren't there." He shrugged. "Right?"

"Yes. My family." She looked distant. "I've heard the story so many times I feel like I was there." She gave out a breathy laugh like she was in some black and white romance movie, then told him her family's story.

While cutting into the mountain and setting up the mine, one of her ancestors had found an old metal box. When he opened it, it appeared to be empty.

"Appeared," she said. "But the more skeptical of us— er—them believed he'd let something out."

"What do *you* believe?" Roger asked. He motioned to the dining room and pulled out a chair for her. When she sat down, the scent of cloves and cinnamon wafted off her. Warm and inviting.

The lights were dim like candlelight. It gave her cheeks a flushed look and sparkled in her eyes. He stared at her, fully aware of it, but unable to stop. She settled in the chair and smoothed her skirt.

"I believe something happened, but I don't know if it resulted from opening the box or carving into that mountain."

People in her family changed. They grew violent and angry. Soon they stopped sleeping and did strange things at night. Wandering the hotel and surrounding areas naked. Fearing fire. Speaking in wordless, raspy voices.

A lightning bolt flashed, followed immediately by a thunderclap that shook the large window in the dining room, startling them both.

Gloria had grabbed Roger's hand. Hers was warm and soft. She didn't let go. Neither did he.

"Talking about this puts me on edge," she said.

"Don't worry," Roger said. "It was so long ago."

He changed the subject. He wanted to know more about her, rather than the oddities of her ancestral past. They talked into the night. Though the lightning and thunder had moved on, sideways rain pelted the window, and wind tossed the trees.

A few moments of silence gathered around them. Roger looked at his watch. It was almost midnight.

"May I," Gloria started. She met his eyes through her lashes. "May I stay in the hotel tonight?"

Roger raised an eyebrow at her.

"I live alone and these storms frighten me so." She took a quick breath. "I'll pay."

Roger smiled. "No need," he said. "Happy to accommodate a member of a local historical family." He smiled. Gloria did, too, but hers was tentative and didn't fully reach her eyes, almost as if she weren't sure if he was being facetious or honest. "Pick a room."

Gloria rose to her feet. "The room at the end of the hall upstairs is nice," she said. "They all are, but that one is my favorite."

Roger motioned for her to lead the way through the dining room entry to the cozy lobby. He bustled around the counter.

"If you would please sign in," he said with a flourish at the register book. "I'll have your key ready."

She gave him a genuine smile this time and picked up the pen. While she scribbled in the book, he turned around and pulled the key for her room from the hook. Attached to it was an obnoxiously large—he knew it—brass tag with the room number on it.

He handed Gloria her key.

"Would you like me to show you up?" he asked.

"That would be lovely," Gloria said.

Roger held out his elbow, and she took it. He guided her to the stairs and up, pointing out bits of architecture he had borrowed from the old hotels during the construction of the first transcontinental railroad. At the top, he pointed out the manager's quarters to the right of the stairs before turning left and taking her down the hall.

At the end of the hall, he unlocked her door for her and waved her in.

"Have a lovely night, Ms. Firestone," he said.

"Thank you, Mr. Alaster." Amusement shined in her eyes. An almost overwhelming urge to kiss her goodnight— a quick peck on the cheek; he was a gentleman after all— overcame him.

He cleared his throat and took a step back. "Please, call me Roger."

Tucked away in her room, Roger returned to the first floor and finished tidying up from the grand opening celebration. It was well past midnight when he'd finished making a loaf of banana bread to serve with some purchased pastries for breakfast. For Gloria, or whoever might stop in, even if it were to tell him what a mistake he'd made.

All while he worked, he thought of Gloria upstairs sleeping, and the story she'd told him. After their long talk, he'd forgotten about the flash change of her face, and by this time, he dismissed it as a trick of the low light, and the strobe effect of the lights flickering.

He turned off the light in the kitchen and dining room and went upstairs. At the top, he looked down the hallway, lit by glowing sconces, toward Gloria's room, before going into his own.

Later that night, a loud thump out in the hall awakened him. He sat bolt upright, heart pounding, mouth dry. At the bottom of the door, two shadows split the line of light coming in from the hall sconces.

They stopped sleeping. Gloria's voice echoed in his mind. *They wandered the halls of the hotel and surrounding areas naked.*

He suddenly regretted not opting for peepholes in the doors.

"Gloria?" he said, but his voice came out in a whisper. He tried again. "Gloria, is that you?"

It had to be. He locked the front door, and no one had rung the bell.

As if on cue, the bell—which only rang to his room and the lobby—dinged.

Roger jumped. He froze, waiting. It dinged again. He rubbed his face and went to the desk in the corner to look at the security camera for the front door. No one was there, but a shadow lurked just on the periphery.

Probably some stupid kids pranking. Ding-dong ditch bull crap. Finally, a figure stepped into the light and rang the bell again.

The man was naked, whoever it was, and held something under one arm. Something rectangular. He set it on the porch and looked up at the camera. Roger didn't recognize him. The man stepped backward off the porch and out of the frame.

The two shadows under Roger's door had vanished.

He pulled on a pair of jeans and stepped into the hallway. Gloria's door was closed and there was no one in the hall. Roger descended the stairs.

In the lobby, he turned on the light and sidled to the front door. There were two windows flanking it, covered by lace curtains. He peeked out.

No one was there.

Rain slanted down in the porch's light.

Roger unlocked the deadbolt and doorknob and cracked the door open.

A rusty metal box sat on the welcome mat. Roger peered into the darkness out on the vacant street.

It could have been the rain mixed with a slight wind rustling the trees, but he thought he could hear voices rasping in the dark. Roger cocked an ear.

Falling rain, rustling bushes, rasping voices all likely sounded the same at three in the morning. He picked up the box and went inside where he set it on the front desk to deal with in the morning.

At the bottom of the stairs, he paused, remembering Gloria's story once again. He went back to the box and lifted it. He gave it a vigorous shake.

It seemed to be—

When he opened it, it appeared to be empty. Gloria's voice again.

A shudder went through him again. He dared not open it. Or did he?

"Come on, Rodge," he whispered to himself. "It's an old family myth of hers. She said herself she'd heard it so many times it was like she was there herself. Who's to say the story hasn't changed all these years later?"

A simple clasp held the box shut, like a military storage box.

Held shut. Like it was keeping something in.

Roger shook his head at his own silliness, fingered the latch, but did not lift it. He hesitated for a few breathless moments, then flipped it up. He flung the lid open.

Nothing. Empty. Not even a windy whoosh of some ill demon escaping.

A scream came from upstairs.

Roger abandoned the box and took the stairs two at a time. He stopped and looked down the long hallway.

"Gloria?" he shouted. The door to her room stood open. Beyond the threshold was penetrating darkness.

Roger dry swallowed the lump in his throat.

"Gloria?" he called again, his voice small and afraid. He took a couple slow and halting steps forward.

Rasping voices came from the black and gaping maw of her room. Voices, plural. Not just one.

The lights flickered and went out.

Roger swallowed a scream. He groped for the wall, the handrail, and ran down the stairs, tripped on the rug at the bottom, and sprawled onto his chest. He crawled, scrambling for the lobby desk to get his bearings. There, he grasped the desk like a lifesaver and listened hard, while simultaneously fumbling for the desk drawers. He'd purchased a box of candles for no apparent reason—at the time—but with no flashlight close at hand, they were his only option. He blindly fluttered his hands around, sure he'd put them in the top drawer. His eyes remained fixed on the stairs.

Just as his hand found the rough corner of the cardboard box of candles, the bell rang.

Roger's head shot from the dark stairway to the front door. He froze. Ice climbed his spine.

The streetlamps out on the road were still lit, and by their dull light, he could see figures peering in through the lace curtains, hands cupped around their faces.

Some crazy townsperson had cut the power and was now there to harass him to prove some stupid point. And Gloria, dear sweet beautiful Gloria, must have been in on it.

Fuming, Roger abandoned the hunt for candles and stomped to the front door.

He tore aside the lace curtain.

Clancy, naked as the day he was born, a wide and toothy grin stretched across his face, peered in. Only his eyes shifted. They swiveled to look at Roger, to meet Roger's eyes.

Roger cried out and stumbled back. He checked the other side. Old Bill Shay. Out on the street, a crowd of similarly undressed elder folks stood with stooped shoulders and slightly bent knees, limp arms hanging by their sides.

And they all smiled.

"Mr. Alaster," Gloria's voice said behind him.

Roger whirled away from the window. She was at the bottom of the stairs, fully dressed and looking as sweet as could be. Behind her, however, stood two people who had the stretched and tanned skin of the ancient mummies he'd seen at an exhibit in Denver not too long ago. They were naked and quietly rasping.

Roger shook his head, brow furrowed in anger. He breathed rapidly through his flared nostrils.

"Oh, this is some joke, isn't it," he stated. "I see now. They hired you, didn't they." His questions weren't questions. He nodded.

"Whatever do you mean?" Gloria asked, still calm. Still pleasant.

Roger mocked her. "*Whatever do you mean?*" He scoffed. "Drop the act. You got me." He raised his hands in surrender, then flung them forward in dismissal.

The mummified men shifted on the stairs. Gloria held them back with her arm.

"Who are your friends?" Roger asked casually as he made his way to the desk. "Great makeup. You sneak them in here during the open house?" He pulled out a candle and lit it with a match from one of the promotional matchbooks he'd put on the counter. He set the candle on the counter by the register book.

The mummies shrank back with agitated rasps.

"Mr. Alaster. I must insist you put the fire out." Gloria reached a hand forward.

"No. I don't think I will," Roger said. Instead, he pulled out another candle and lit it, and another. He lined them up on the desk and cast a glance toward the windows. Clancy and Old Bill Shay's faces were gone. He wondered if the crowd in the street had dispersed.

He lifted the rusted metal box.

"Who'd you get to deliver this?" he asked.

Gloria gasped and dropped onto the bottom step.

"No! No!" she cried. "That's the box!" Her voice had gone all shrieky. She hid her face in her hands, her voice blubbering from behind them. "I wondered why they'd shown up." She sobbed into her palms.

When she looked up again, the demonic flicker he'd seen when they were talking in the kitchen replaced her beauty. "You opened it." Her voice dropped several octaves.

She lunged to her feet and flew at him. A few candles fell over. One lit her sleeve, but it didn't stop her from latching her hands around Roger's neck.

Roger pulled at her fingers, bent them back, until she cried out with a demonic bass voice and released him. Roger ran to the front door, fumbled at the locks, and jerked it open.

Smoke billowed out of the hotel behind him. Roger coughed and stumbled forward down the porch steps. He looked behind him, still backing away. The lobby was on fire. Gloria and her mummy friends were nowhere to be seen.

When he turned back around, the naked elderly still stood around, unmoving, and, as if they'd been waiting for this moment, they all shifted their eyes to look at him.

Roger took hesitant steps. Their eyes followed. A few at a time twitched. A head jerk here. A shoulder lift there.

The hardware store owner stepped out from behind Leeta, fully clothed.

"We warned you," he said.

"What the hell is going on?" Roger cried, stepping closer to the only other sane person, reaching out to him for a lifeline.

The rasping started at the edges of the group.

"Is this some kind of joke to drive me out? Tell me what's going on!" He all but shook the man.

"You didn't listen," the hardware store owner said. "You came here and forced your way in. You were friendly, trying to belong. As if friendliness is all it took to be one of us." He spat on the ground.

"I inherited that land! It belongs to my family. I forced nothing."

"You want to be one of us?" the man asked. He took a menacing step toward Roger, who backed away in tandem. "You want to belong?"

The naked elderly attacked, piling on top of him with their saggy flesh hitting him from all sides. Roger cried out to the hardware store owner to no effect.

In the background, his brand-new hotel went up in flames. The windows exploded outward, showering the street with glass.

The elderly lifted him like he was crowd surfing. Roger squirmed, fighting to get away, but their bony fingers only dug in deeper. The rasping increased in volume as they carried him away from the fire and into the woods surrounding the town.

They marched for at least a quarter-mile, if not farther. Roger never stopped struggling until they put him down at the base of the mountain. The dark condemned entry to the mine was a black mouth against the night. Cold and stenchy air wafted out of it like a crypt.

He supposed it probably was.

The hardware store owner shackled Roger to two posts and disappeared in the wall of wrinkled flesh without a word.

"Hey," Roger hollered. The elderly turned as one and shuffled off into the trees.

The glow of his hotel on fire lit up the night.

Roger hung his head.

After a time, a twig snapped. He looked up.

"Gloria?" Roger said, bewildered at the sight of her, perfect again. No sign of burns or evil. "How?"

She came closer to him. Close enough to smell her clove and cinnamon scent.

"I was there," she said. "I was there when my ancestors —my family—opened the box." She gazed upward, presumably at the mountain towering behind him. "I've never loved this place." Moonlight sparkled in her eyes.

Rasping issued from behind Roger. He turned his head to look, but couldn't see directly behind him, where the mouth to the mine gaped. The first few mummies shuffled into his periphery a few seconds later and gathered behind Gloria.

"This is my family," she said in a choked whisper. "We belong to the mountain. To the mine."

"Why am I here like this?" Roger asked. "I didn't do anything wrong!"

Gloria touched his cheek.

"You set fire to the hotel."

"It was an accident," Roger said, then thought twice. "You're the one who knocked the candles over."

Gloria shook her head and pressed a finger to his lips. "Not that hotel." She caressed his cheek. "The one you built before. When you were Monty. Montgomery Alaster."

Roger didn't understand. He shook his head, confused.

"Your past life, Roger."

"Montgomery was my great-great-grandfather."

She shook her head. "That's what you want to believe. But you know, deep down you know." She stepped even closer to him. "I can see it in the way you look at me. In the way you replicated your old hotel as if to call us all back."

Roger didn't have a clue what she was talking about.

"Guilt carries on through lifetimes. As does love." She touched his face with her delicate fingers. "We were lovers." She gazed into his eyes. "You burned your own hotel to rid me of my husband, so you and I could be together." She looked away in that coquettish way of hers, then met his eyes again. "But it was against my wishes."

She stepped back among the mummies. "I was in the hotel, too."

Roger still didn't understand.

"Now, you are cursed to relive the same story, life after life, always returning here to build again."

"This is crazy," Roger shouted, struggling against the shackles.

"I'm here to end your suffering. To end the curse." She looked around at the naked mummies. "We can finally be together." She came near again and kissed him.

Her lips tasted bitter and within moments he sagged against his bonds and darkness overcame him.

Roger awoke in the woods, curled in the fetal position between the posts. Someone had removed his shackles. It was still dark, but the sky was no longer orange with fire. He got to his feet but really had nowhere to go. His hotel—and therefore residence—burned down. His life savings, gone. Everything he'd done to make a life for himself, ruined.

As he wandered back toward town, his skin itched and burned. He struggled out of his shirt, then his undershirt. The cool night air touched his skin but didn't ease the sensations. He stripped off his pants, socks, underwear. Still, his skin itched. He stopped and looked back at the trail of clothes.

His head jerked. His shoulder lifted.

And then he rasped.

She cleaned their house twice a week, sometimes more if a celebration had been in order. Celebrations like *we made it through Monday, it's Thursday.* Things like that.

Dozens of beer bottles, wine bottles, spent cigarette butts, and other types of smokes littered every flat surface. Crushed snacks stained the carpet with orange pollen.

They were pigs. Every one of them. Sometimes they still slept when she arrived. She'd knock to announce her presence. Bang pots and pans so they knew she was there. Vacuum despite the soft snores coming from cracked bedroom doors where they slept with reckless abandon, limbs thrown in every direction, naked bodies piled so high she couldn't tell where one stopped and another started.

Filthy pigs.

She chuckled softly as she drained the can of gasoline across the entryway. It would be the best pig roast in the world.

Dream Hitchhiker

Sometimes when I dream, I feel someone else there with me. Someone on the edges of my periphery. A persistence of vision trick where, when you look, the thing you think you saw disappears. When I wake from these dreams, I feel a weird sense of violation. Like someone else has seen into my soul and into the very depths of who I am.

Though my dreams aren't frightening, those days after the Dream Hitchhiker is there, I feel like I can't scrub away that creeping feeling. What does it want? Why did it pick me? It puts me ill at ease.

I want to have nightmares. The bad ones I used to have as a kid. If the Dream Hitchhiker can come along on that ride, I think it would go away and leave me alone for good.

I eat candy and cookies and ice cream right before bed, hoping it will cause bad dreams to come.

Driving off cliffs because of failing brakes.

Navigating through a world of lava and fiery explosions.

Falling from high places.

Bites from rabid animals.

The chaos of trying to get people to listen to me when everyone is yelling about something else. Something unrelated.

They don't sound scary on the outside, but when you dream them, there is an added element of not being in control that seals the fear inside.

I dream. The Hitchhiker is there with me. The dream starts out innocuous but quickly shifts gears. I'm in a house, then suddenly I'm in a car. It's night. The headlights are shining on a dirt road speeding by. I'm behind the wheel, but from the back seat, trying to drive an out-of-control car. Curtains separating the front from the back swing shut, then open, then shut again with the jostling of the car on the potholed road.

The headlights flicker.

The headlights go out.

I hear a yell.

"Stop the car," the voice shouts. It's an unearthly voice. One made of sleep essence and paralysis.

"I can't," I say, matter-of-factly.

"Let me out," the Hitchhiker says.

"I can't." I grin. I've carried this fool into the lucid state with me. I am in control now. "You have to ride it out."

A scaly clawed hand grabs the headrest of the front passenger seat, grips it. If it were human, the knuckles would be white.

The dream jumps again. It's daylight, and we are careening down a steep hill on a paved road, heading straight for a cliff. If I can't slow the car to navigate the turn at the bottom, we'll fly off into oblivion. I know I will wake before we hit—I always do—but the Dream Hitchhiker does not.

"The brakes are out," I tell it. "Brace yourself."

A savage scream rips from its throat, pure terror as if all the world's nightmares—real and imagined—explode from its vocal cords.

The car rockets over the edge.

I shake myself awake and momentarily smile to myself for a job well done.

Then I hear the rapid respirations of a terrified being. I turn my head and the Dream Hitchhiker lays in bed next to me, gripping the sheets.

A New Set of Ears

The day had come. Edward would finally hear again. The class-action suit against the machine company he'd worked for over half his life had finally settled, granting him enough money to afford the ears he saw at Parts 'R' Us. They were sitting in a glass case next to a hand with a beautiful diamond ring on it. A guy at the counter was inquiring about the hand. No, about the ring. Apparently, it was his fiancé's hand.

Edward purchased the ears and took them to the surgeon who promised he could get them attached and working properly so Eddie—as the doctor called him, much to Edward's disapproval—could hear again. The doctor seemed reputable. The hospital did, too. It was one of those big hospitals that do all manner of things. Emergencies, surgeries, long-term care probably. Occupational therapies. Rehab. The works.

On the day of surgery, Edward gave the front desk his form. The lady's mouth moved. He pointed to his ears and shook his head with a shrug.

The woman nodded, understanding. She wrote down the floor number. It was minus three.

Edward boarded the elevator and hit the minus three button.

He never even saw Dr. Rickard before he went under.

Edward woke from surgery as anyone might. Groggy, shivering, cold to his core. A little weepy from the anesthesia. But, got-damn! He could hear. He could hear the guy on the bed next door yelling for water and groaning a god-awful agonizing moan. He could hear the machines beeping, the nurses bustling about.

Someone whispered directly into his right ear. Edward jerked his head in that direction. Bad idea. Wooziness overtook him. He closed his eyes and drifted back into oblivion once more.

When he woke again, he was in a different place. A private room with a TV up on the wall and a window, which surprised him since he was underground mere hours ago.

He was still in mild shock at the fact that, when he moved his legs under the scratchy starchy blankets, he could hear the susurration. He laughed out loud, then covered his mouth.

Though he hadn't been born deaf, he hadn't heard a thing in at least fifteen years. Maybe longer, since it was a gradual deafening.

"La la la," he whispered. Then louder and louder until he belted out the note like an operatic singer with laryngitis. He ended the drawn-out warbly tone with a fit of coughing and another laugh.

A nurse poked her head in. "Everything okay?" Her voice was bright and sonorous to his new ears.

"Yes," he said. "Everything is just incredible."

She grinned at him. "We'll be in to check your vitals in a bit, hon."

He checked out of the hospital that afternoon after Dr. Rickard came in to ensure everything was in order. He did a quick hearing test with the high- and low-pitched beeps. Edward scored one hundred percent. He'd never scored one hundred percent, not even when he was much younger. As a result, he bleated out another involuntary laugh.

"Sounds like you're pleased with the results," Dr. Rickard said, closing Edward's file. He gave Edward a satisfactory grin. "You'll rate us five stars on the old Googles, wontcha Eddie?"

"Yes, yes I will," Edward said. The doctor winked at him and left the room. Edward got dressed and waited for the nurse to come to discharge him.

When he got home, his cat greeted him at the door with a series of yowls. Edward had never heard his cat before. Tiger was a rescue, and, despite what her name implied, she was a Siamese.

"Don't you have a powerful voice." Edward patted the cat's head. Her purrs vibrated against his new ears. It was the most wondrous of sounds. Edward spent the rest of the day listening to his favorite records, which had collected dust over the years. Jazz, mostly, a little reggae, and a few symphonies he'd had the pleasure of hearing live ages ago.

He sat in his favorite chair with Tiger purring on his lap and listened, head leaned against the back of the chair. It was the most amazing thing.

That night, as he lay in bed, Tiger jumped up with a

trilling *miaow* and settled next to him. He stroked her silky fur. The sounds of his apartment building settling clicked and *thunked* around him. The refrigerator kicked on, adding white noise. Then it kicked off and everything seemed muffled and quieter. Edward tossed and turned. He'd only lived in the place for about nine years. He didn't know how noisy it was. People talking on the street below, cars whooshing by, rain puddles splashing under tires. A siren. A high-pitched laugh.

Edward taco-ed his head in his pillow. He finally dozed off when someone, again, whispered directly into his right ear.

He sat up straight and looked around, heart pounding. It wasn't a word or anything he recognized. Just the sibilant sound of a whisper. Edward strained to hear, in case it was someone out in the hall or something, whispering as they made their way to their own apartment, but he didn't hear it again.

He lay back, wide awake now. He coiled Tiger's tail around his fingers. It flicked and fluttered and got away from him, then lashed the comforter. But still, she purred. He focused on that rumbling vibration. The sound eased him back toward slumber.

On the edges of sleep, in that lucid state in which one knows one is dreaming and tries desperately to wake up in the event of a nightmare, a hiss began deep within his mind. It increased in volume, but not intensity, always keeping a whispery quality to it.

He flopped over onto his side.

"Goddamn faulty ears," he mumbled. When he spoke, his own voice echoed about a half-second off. Like someone was mocking him while he spoke. Someone in the room with him, listening to him.

Edward sat up so abruptly, Tiger shot off the bed with a startled scream.

"Who's there?" he yelled into his dark apartment. No one answered. He strained again to hear, to catch the sound. He couldn't be sure if it had been a dream or not. "Hello?" he said, testing. No echo. It *must* have been a dream.

Edward settled back again, but he was wide awake now, worried his new ears were defective. He tossed and turned, thinking about calling Dr. Rickard to find out if this was normal. Perhaps his brain was just getting used to this returned sense that had been lost so long ago. Sensory overload or something.

He dragged himself out of bed the next morning, tired as hell. Tiger curled around his legs as he made his way to the kitchen to make coffee. While the grinder buzzed obnoxiously loud—Edward winced against the sound—he thought he heard people talking. As soon as he stopped the noise, though, they stopped, too.

"White noise phenomenon of some sort," he muttered. He ran water in the sink, filling the coffeepot, and heard the noise again.

After two cups of coffee and a read-through of the paper, Edward got on the horn with Dr. Rickard's office. The phone rang and rang, and no one answered. Not even an answering service or voicemail. He grumbled and hung up after the twenty-ninth ring and did an internet search.

He tried several search terms and finally found something that caught his interest.

Woman with cochlear implants hears the beyond.

Edward scoffed. "The beyond? Can you believe that Tigey?" He cooed at his cat and scratched under her chin.

She peered at him with her bright blue crossed eyes, tail lashing, purr vibrating.

He clicked the link.

Madeline Streya had lost her ears in some attack back when places like Parts 'R' Us and the Organ Library started acquiring and selling such "merchandise." She wrote about how she searched for her ears but couldn't find them. Finally, she got new ears, and that's when she started hearing voices from the beyond and dedicated the rest of her life to helping others experiencing similar situations.

She sounded looney as fuck. But after reading her entire website, he clicked on the Contact Me tab, entered his information, and wrote a brief note.

Got new ears the other day. Can't sleep. Every time I try, I hear whispers. Heard of this?

He submitted the contact form and peered out the glass door onto his balcony. Tiger played in the vertical blinds. They clacked together each time she swatted and pounced.

Edward jumped when his laptop dinged with a new email. It was from the crazy lady.

Dear Edward,

Thank you so much for reaching out. I got your message from my website submission form.

Tiger jumped up on his desk and pawed at his hand. He absently stroked her from top to tail.

I would love to meet with you to discuss this phenomenon you are experiencing. I know face to face is odd in this day of technology, but I feel it is important we connect. Please let me know when a good time for you is.

Edward hit reply but hesitated. She was a stranger. He should be careful. There were a lot of scams going on over emails and texts and the like.

Hello,

Would you be open to a video call instead? Also, how much is this going to cost me?

He hadn't seen any pricing info on her website and wondered if she was going to charge him and how much it would set him back. He'd just spent a bundle on these new ears. He hit send.

A response came a few minutes later.

A video call would be superb. Can you meet now? This won't cost a thing.

This wouldn't cost a thing. What was it, a free consultation? Edward hit reply and said yes. She forwarded him some video call details.

Edward plugged in his old Jabra headset, signed on to the conference call, and adjusted his camera and the lighting while he waited for Madeline to join. Tiger jumped on the desk and pawed at his hand resting on the mouse.

Finally, her face appeared on a background of dark grays and misty whites. She must have had some privacy filter on her background or something. Her long red hair framed her face. Definitely the same woman from the website.

"Face to face *is* odd in this day of technology, isn't it?" she said with a breathy laugh Edward liked the sound of. "Thank you for meeting with me virtually." She shifted in her chair. "When did you get them?" she asked, pointing at her own ears.

"Yesterday-ay." Edward's voice echoed that half-second behind. "I think the connection is bad-ad. I can hear myself-elf. Let me leave and come back-ack." He did that to no avail. "It must be my old headset. This thing is a dinosaur-or." He shrugged. "I'll manage-age."

Madeline nodded. "Can you pull your headset to the side and show me your ears?"

Edward did as asked, moving closer so she could see them in his camera. He turned his head from one side to the other.

"They're obviously real, not man-made, and I mean that in a kind way. The man-made ones are subpar in my opinion. It's hard these days to find cadaver implants," Madeline said. "Where did you get them?"

He felt foolish that he got the ears from such a shady part of town and such a seedy little store, but sighed and said, "I got them from Parts 'R' Us." His voice echoed.

Madeline nodded without judgment. "And what have you heard?"

Edward huffed a mirthless laugh. "Aside from every loud-mouthed asshole in my building and every car that drives by on the street below, there's this whisper. I also heard voices this morning when grinding coffee and filling the coffeepot with water from the noisy tap-ap."

She nodded along with what he was saying. "When did it start?"

"Before I even left the hospital. I heard it the first time in the recovery room. Right into my right ear, like someone had their mouth right up against it, without the tickle of warm breath, of course-ourse."

"Very peculiar," she said. "I've never heard of it happening that fast."

"Never heard of what happening this fast-ast?" Edward asked.

She didn't answer his question but asked another of her own. "What do the whispers say?"

Edward shrugged. "Nothing. It's just sound-ound."

"And when you try to hear more?"

"Silence-ence." He'd gotten used to the echo. "What

have you never heard of happening this fast-ast?" he inquired again.

"The messages," she said in a low and mystical voice. She paused and leaned forward. Edward leaned forward, too, despite himself. "From beyond."

He sat back with a scoff that echoed in his headset. It was a sound he would never make again.

"I know it's hard to believe," Madeline went on. "But there is a place between the worlds of life and death. It's like a waiting room for the soul. The soul and the body maintain some sort of, well, spiritual link until the soul moves on from this realm," she said. "The ears—your ears—have heard things. *Are* hearing things. Things the soul is experiencing in that nebulous area between life and death."

"This is ludicrous. Thanks for your time-ime." He lifted his hands to his headset.

"No, please," Madeline said holding out her hands in a halting gesture.

Edward had nothing else to do, and he did like the sound of her voice. It had a soothing quality after all the rambunctiousness of his block in the heart of the city.

"Let me make sure I understand … what you're trying to tell me, is that you believe what I'm hearing is something that the previous owner—or his or her spirit anyway—is hearing now, in whatever afterlife limbo there may be-ee?"

Madeline nodded her head as he spoke, a smile on her lips, eyebrows raised in excitement.

"Well, guess what, lady, I don't believe in the afterlife-ife." He reached again for his headset.

"There's only one way to stop the whispers," she said. "I can help you."

Edward lowered his hands again. "Tell me-ee."

"You have to really relax. If you can relax and not

react to the whisper, the ears will tell you what the soul needs. What it wants. And once you find that out, you can help it traverse the plain to the true afterlife." She spoke in that mystical voice of hers.

"Like meditation-shun," Edward stated. He'd never been good at sitting still. He itched to move around, get things done. Sitting and doing nothing was a waste of time that could be spent doing things.

"Exactly," Madeline said. "We need to make sure your environment is quiet. Maybe go to the quietest room in your apartment?"

Edward laughed. It echoed. Not a bad laugh. "That would be the bathroom-oom."

"Are you on a laptop? Can you … um … take me in there with you?" She shook her head as if realizing it was a strange request.

Edward nodded. He unplugged his docking station and carried the laptop into the bathroom.

"I will guide you this first time, teach you the techniques to use on your own. I have a booklet. I can email the PDF version."

"How much is this going to cost-ost?" Edward asked.

Madeline laughed. A delightful sound. "Not a thing." She grinned. "I'm always curious to hear what my clients hear. It feeds my fascination with the beyond and the way our world interacts with theirs."

He settled on the floor in front of the toilet with his laptop on the closed lid, and followed her voice, doing what she asked as she gave him instructions.

"Let me know when the ears speak," Madeline whispered.

Edward kept taking deep breaths. His mind wandered, and finally, the whisper came.

"There it is," he whispered, ignoring the echo. "Just the sound. No words yet."

"Keep listening," Madeline said. "Focus without focusing."

He had no idea what that meant but tried to do what she said.

At the end of the session, Edward didn't get anywhere. She told him to keep practicing, that maybe the headset interfered or something. She said the ears would tell him what he needed to know before too long. He just had to let them know he was listening. An open vessel to their messages.

A week later, Edward emailed Madeline. He hadn't heard the strange echoing since their video call, and he hadn't gotten anywhere with focusing without focusing to hear what the ears wanted to tell him. They agreed to meet at a small park outside of the city. One that wasn't frequented often and guaranteed to be quiet.

The outdoors might invoke the voices, she explained in her email response.

Fresh air, sounds of nature, all things that can help you ease into the listening state. This park is also a place of powerful energy. I'm drawn there often, sometimes without even realizing I've wandered there.

Edward could hear her breathy laugh through her written words.

On the day and time they arranged to meet, Edward found himself not at a park, but at a cemetery. Madeline stood under a large oak tree, her back to him. The wind lifted her fiery red hair and played with the hem and sleeves of her gauzy dress. She looked stunning.

Edward shook his head and approached.

"Madeline-lin." He stuck a finger in his ear. The echo was back.

"Have a seat," she said, indicating a grassy patch beneath the tree.

Edward sat. Madeline sat in front of him cross-legged. She tucked her dress around her legs.

"Comfy?" she asked when she looked up at him.

He nodded.

"Good. Now, begin." She dipped her chin once.

He raised an eyebrow at her. She raised both of her eyebrows and nodded at him in a go-ahead-don't-mind-me kind of way.

Edward closed his eyes and took a few deep breaths, settling into the practice she'd taught him.

After a couple of minutes, the sound in his ears changed. A low rush began, like static on a TV turned down to a quarter of its volume level.

It's me, a voice whispered.

Edward startled and opened his eyes.

"What? What is it?" Madeline asked, sitting forward with her hands pressed against her knees.

"I heard words this time-ime," he said. "It's me, they said-ed."

"We have to find out who 'it' is."

He sank back into the deep breaths, focusing on the words he'd heard and an intention to find out what the message was. His mind was distracted by possibilities. He refocused, thinking over and over again, *who are you?*

Me.

Edward startled again, losing the connection. Madeline was gripping her elbows now, nibbling on the end of her thumbnail, staring intently at him.

"Me," he said. "The whisper said, me."

Madeline nodded. "Okay. Okay." She bit her thumb nail. "Keep trying." She waved her hand in a circle in a get-on-with-it gesture.

Edward glanced at his watch before closing his eyes again. They'd been at it for two and a half hours. Tiger would be hungry soon. She was probably already yowling for her dinner.

He focused this time on *who are you?*

After what felt like a lot longer time than before, the voice spoke again.

Madeline.

Edward's eyes popped open. Madeline still had her thumb in her teeth. A tiny bit of blood had run into the cracks on either side of her nail. Her eyes had worry lines all around them.

"What?" she asked around her thumb. "What did they say?" Tears gathered in her eyes.

Edward took a deep breath and gripped his knees. He looked up at the leaves gently rustling in the branches above. Their sibilant sounds similar to the whispers from "the beyond." He thought about the echoing. How he only experienced it when Madeline was around either virtually or here in person. Because he was hearing himself the way she heard him.

He looked at the fading sunlight dappling Madeline's face. Where the light touched her, she became translucent, her skin flickering in and out of existence.

"Madeline." He said. "I think I have *your* ears."

The tears sliding down her cheeks sparkled in the dapples of sunlight shifting on her face. She looked real— physical. He wanted to touch her to see if his hand would pass through her.

"I wasn't sure, but I thought I might have died," she said in that whimsical way of hers. "But I was still here, on this plane. Interacting … with you."

He remembered the echo that first night when he

thought his ears were faulty. "You were in my home … the night I got home from the hospital."

"I felt compelled to walk. I don't know how, but I found myself in your apartment. You were sleeping. When you woke up, I fled." She told him this as if he wouldn't find it creepy—dead *or* alive. "The link between the soul and the body, remember? My soul knew where to find you because of the ears." She looked away and back. "Because of *my* ears."

They sat quietly for a time. Edward didn't know what to say. He felt numb. Then he laughed.

"You said you were drawn here, to this place, because of the energy or some mumbo jumbo, right?"

She nodded.

"Maybe you were buried here."

They spent an hour scouring the cemetery for Madeline's grave. They finally found it in a nice spot full of sunlight. They stared down at her tombstone. Just her name and the obligatory dates. She hadn't died that long ago. The ground was still mounded, though some grass had grown.

Edward cleared his throat. It echoed in his ears. "Are there any other messages you need to tell me?" He met her eyes. "So you can move on, I mean."

"No," she mouthed. No sound came out inside or outside of his ears. She kneeled in front of her tombstone and wept. Little by little she faded away.

"Good luck," Edward said, not sure what else to say. Then, she was gone.

Edward looked around the empty cemetery, wondering for the first time in his life how many other souls were there, standing by, waiting. Drawn there by the power of the place. The energy, as Madeline had said.

As he shuffled to his car, he found he was a little sad.

Wacky as hell she might have been, but he loved her voice, her laugh, the emails they passed back and forth …

He drove home in silence.

That night, as he lay in bed petting Tiger and listening to the ocean waves crashing on the white noise machine he'd purchased to block out the sounds from the street below, someone whispered in his *left* ear.

Organan Library

Donations were accepted every Thursday when the surgeon was available to catalog and check in the parts for more *organ*ized—pun intended—processing. He used that joke more than necessary.

His favorites to handle were hearts and brains. He hated hands and feet. The *grotesqueness* of phalanges frozen in death—

A donor stumbled in on his last legs—the legs he checked out the last time he came in—his arm over his belly.

"New shipment," he wheezed. The surgeon helped him onto the table and opened the donor's blood-stained jacket. He removed the unconnected parts inside the donor's body cavity.

"Brain, stomach—" he swallowed hard. "A foot."

The surgeon decided, because of the foot of course, to take the heart, too, even though it was still attached.

The Black Dog Comes Out of the Corn

It doesn't matter how I get there, but once I'm there, I know, because the entry is always the same. A dark tunnel that ends inside the walls of a house I've never seen or been to outside of my dreams. An old house that has lath and plaster walls. The plaster has crumbled off in large sections. Me and whatever friend has come with me can see through the thin slats at what's happening inside the house, but I can never remember that part. I just remember the fear. How frightening it is to be inside the wall, semi exposed. In the dream, I even wonder how the people inside can't see us. And maybe that's where the terror comes from. Hiding without being hidden.

The dream always ends the same. The "camera" pans away from the house, which is at the edge of a huge end-of-season cornfield. The cornstalks are tall and yellow and dried out. The house looms above, as if on a hill. It looks out of place there with the sun shining down on the golden cornstalks.

As the camera zooms out, and as wakefulness comes to

bundle me out of the dream world, a black dog trots—in slow motion—out of the corn. The corn doesn't move.

It's terrifying for no reason, really. Scary in the way dreams just sometimes are. I wake covered in sweat, eyes swiveling around the room in anticipation of seeing *something,* some remnant from the dream, left behind in my physical world. It's a dream whose hold of terror diffuses once told out loud to anyone.

"I guess it's not *that* scary," I said after telling the first rendition to a friend. I got to the house through a cave after beaching a Viking ship on the shore. There were bodiless heads flying down a cave tunnel, spinning and wailing. I got inside the walls of the house to hide from them.

But now, when I have this dream, this nightmare, the horror follows me out of it. Because after every time I dream it, someone I know—the person with me *in* the dream—dies horribly.

I had the dream last night, only this time, I was alone. I woke feeling relief. No one would die today.

But as I lay in bed thinking, *I wonder if it will be me*, I break out in a cold sweat and sit up slowly, running my hands over my face and hair. Chills have raised goosebumps on my arms and legs. I shiver.

I'm supposed to go to a site today to analyze an old house to see if it qualifies as historical. On my way there, I take extra precautions and mindfully take my time to get there.

When I pull up and see the place for the first time, my

mouth goes dry. It looks like the one from the dream. Beyond the house is a cornfield.

A tremor makes my knees feel weak. I hold on to my car for a moment. The person from the historical society, who agreed to meet me at the site, is sitting on the front porch. She rises with a smile on her face.

"Thank you so much for coming," she says as she approaches down the long path from the front door. She holds out her hand, but when our eyes meet, her smile falters. "Are you okay?" she asks.

I nod but don't speak. Not yet. I'm afraid of what sound might come out. I clear my throat a few times. "Yes, yes. I'm okay. Nice to meet you in person. Sarah, was it?"

"Yes."

"Todd." I finally shake her hand. She surreptitiously wipes her palm on her skirt afterward. I don't blame her. My hands are sweating, and it isn't from the sun beating down on us.

"Shall we?" She motions to the house.

I follow her up the path, dread filling every crack and crevice of my body with each step toward that front door.

Based on the state of the foundation and exterior walls, I can already tell it likely won't qualify as a historical building. A site perhaps, if something significant happened here.

Inside, I survey the entryway. It's a wreck of crumbling plaster and lath walls. This place should be condemned. I loosen my tie and undo the top button on my shirt. I follow Sarah around while she points out details of the house that have remained intact and other areas that could easily be restored … with the right budget. She gives me a smile as if I'm the bank.

At one point, I lose track of her. I'm in the kitchen. There's an old table there in the middle of it. A familiar table I've seen before. In the dream. Usually from the other side of the broken wall.

I glance up and see Sarah peering at me through the exposed laths, eyes smiling.

"Boo," she says with a girlish giggle.

"Get out of there." The words come out harsh and ragged.

"Sorry," she says. "Just having a little fun. There are tunnels in these walls. You should check it out. We could make them secret passageways during the reno."

My stomach has soured. Sweat drips down my ribcage.

"Are you sure you're okay?" she asks me. "You look a little pale."

"Might be coming down with something." I brush past her to leave this godforsaken house. She follows me out.

"When can we expect your decision?" she asks.

I've already decided. The house will be torn down. "In a couple weeks."

She nods. "I hope you'll consider saving it."

I give her a curt nod. She climbs in her car and drives off down the twisting road. I watch her go, and as her car leaves my sight, I double over and wretch onto the gravel driveway.

My entire body is quaking and sweaty. Cold and hot chase each other through my core. I can't seem to get my breath. I just want to get away from there, but I can't possibly drive in this condition.

When the episode fades and my stomach is merely nauseated instead of tossing and turning with sick, I climb into my car and drive down the road in the direction Sarah went. It's the opposite way from how I arrived, but I need to make sure she is okay.

At the bottom of the hill, her car is in the ditch.

On the opposite side of the road is the cornfield. High above, on the hill I'd just drove down, looms the house.

"Oh no. No, no." I pull over behind it and jump out, nearly tumbling into the ditch myself. She's on the road in front of her car, as if she'd somehow hit herself with her own vehicle.

And sliced open her gut.

"Todd." Blood trickles from the corner of her mouth. I drop to my knees next to her and grip her hand.

"What happened?" I ask her, stupidly.

She shakes her head. Tiny movements back and forth. Nearly imperceptible.

It's like Gloria. And Matt. And Roger. Now Sarah.

I hold her in my arms, this virtual stranger, and I stare at the cornstalks, waiting. Knowing.

As she takes her last breaths and slips away from this world, the black dog comes silently out of the corn.

The Other Daughter

Fifteen years since she'd gone missing, and now she stood on my front porch. Unaged. Still a seven-year-old girl with long blonde hair, fair skin, lips too dark to be natural—but they were—and bright blue eyes.

"Hi, Mommy," she said in a bright voice. "I'm home."

I didn't respond right away. I didn't know how. She should be in her early twenties. A woman on the verge of taking on the world.

But this little girl couldn't be my daughter. She looked just like her, but it couldn't be her. Before I could stop her, she pushed her way past me and went to the kitchen where she pulled open the fridge and removed items my girl, my little Samantha, used to love for her afternoon snack.

String cheese. A tube of portable yogurt, which I kept buying even after her disappearance. An apple. She climbed onto the kitchen counter, lithe dancer limbs bending and moving with effortless grace, and retrieved the jar of Nutella from the cupboard above the toaster.

"Mommy, can you help me open this?" She held out

the string cheese. She never could get the "tear here" slit in the top to actually tear.

I took the wrapped cheese from her and opened it, handing it back with the plastic flapped down like an artificial banana peel. She pulled the cylindrical cheese from the wrapper and started pulling fine threads of it off, leaning her head back and dropping them into her mouth. Just like my Samantha.

I moved to the knife block and pulled a knife out of it.

"Let me cut this up for you," I said, moving the apple onto a cutting board. She grinned up at me.

"Thank you, Mommy." She got the top off the tube of yogurt and squeezed it onto a plate. My Samantha never ate it out of the tube either. With all portions of her snack on a plate—I spread Nutella on the apple slices—she pranced into the living room and set it on the ottoman. I turned on her favorite show and shuffled down the hall, hand on my forehead, the other on my chest.

I paused and peeked back into the living room, just to be sure. She was there, fixated on the television, munching away on her apples. She dipped the chocolate spread fruit into the yogurt. I went to the master bedroom and picked up the phone.

When my husband answered, I immediately burst into tears.

"Honey? What is it? Is everything okay?" His voice was full of worried panic.

I got my sobs under control long enough to say, "She's back, Steve. Our baby is back."

Silence.

"Steve? Are you there?"

He cleared his throat. "What did you say?"

"Samantha. She's back."

"I'm coming home."

He arrived a few minutes later since he worked just down the street. He came inside. I stopped him at the door, but Samantha bounded down the hallway. Gliding on her long legs.

"Daddy!" she shouted. She leaped into his arms. Steve held her, his arms on autopilot, but his eyes were wide and fixed on me. I gave him a small shrug.

I hadn't touched Samantha's room since she disappeared, so all her old things were still there, just as she'd left them. I went in once a month to dust, but that was all. She was delighted to find all her things, touching them in awe, as if they were brand new.

By the time we tucked her into bed, my heart had healed almost completely. I turned off her light and hurried to our bedroom, where Steve paced. I closed the door.

He turned toward me. "What the hell is going on?" The question warranted a louder exclamatory voice, but his was a harsh whisper, and I knew it was just something he needed to blurt out. He didn't really expect me to know the answer. "Tell me how this happened."

I shook my head. "She was just … there … on the porch."

"And you let her in? Without question?"

I shook my head. "She just came in. Like she hadn't been missing for so long. Like she forgot the code to the front door and needed me to let her inside."

He paced some more.

"It can't be her, can it? It can't be. Diana, it can't be."

"But it is." I told him about our afternoon together. Every movement, every decision, everything indicated this was our girl.

"She should be, what, twenty-two?"

I nodded.

"We have to ask her what happened. We have to."

"Do we? Can't we just … accept that she's home?"

Steve gave me a sideways look like I'd lost my mind.

"Can we at least wait a few days? Let her get settled?" Though she already had settled, it seemed.

"How are we going to explain this to the neighbors? Our friends? Her friends are all grown up now, she'll want to see them and play with them."

I didn't have answers for him. He didn't expect me to. And, thankfully, as the days went by, Samantha never asked about her friends. I ordered supplies to teach her from home, so we wouldn't have to worry about the school asking questions. We kept to ourselves for the first few weeks.

But Steve had to know what happened.

"Samantha, my little love bug," he said one night while we tucked her into bed. "What happened to you? Where did you go?"

She gave him a quizzical look. "I've been here all along, Daddy. You just didn't see me."

My mouth went dry, and I gulped down the cotton ball knot in my throat.

Steve laughed in the friendly way he did when talking to her. "No, silly. When you were gone for a long time. Where were you?"

She still looked confused. "I don't know."

Another week went by. She was still as smart as she was before she disappeared, speeding through the second-grade class materials and eager to dig into the third-grade books.

One night, however, after we put her to bed, instead of going to our own room on the opposite side of the house, we hung out in the living room. Giggles came from Samantha's room.

"Is she up again?" Steve asked.

I shrugged. "I'll go check on her." I got up and made my way down the dark hallway, careful not to kick any of the toys she'd failed to put away earlier, despite my asking her several times—another behavior so much like my girl from long ago. I slowly opened her door a crack.

From the doorway, I could see the headboard of her bed and her bedside table. The lamp was on, but her beautiful little head was not on her pillow. I opened the door wider.

The thing stood in the middle of her bed in the center of her My Little Pony bedspread. It had a white, featureless face, and two long dangling protrusions, as if—

I chuckled at myself and relaxed a bit.

It was just my little Samantha wearing her old ballet tights on her head.

She hummed random notes while twisting her upper body back and forth, pulling on the protrusions.

"What are you doing up?" I asked, not in a stern voice.

She froze. Her featureless face pointed in my direction. She dropped onto the mattress, butt bouncing, and slung her legs over the edge. She slid off the bed and stood.

As she came nearer, I saw there were features on this blank slate of a face, but they were only a hint of features.

"Take those off and get back in bed," I said, heart beginning to race. I couldn't see the edge of the tights. It should have been there, just under her chin, but it all blended into her neck and disappeared under her nightshirt.

"Take what off, Mommy?" she asked, now twisting back and forth again, the protrusions—the legs of the tights—twirling out to the side and hitting her across the face with each half rotation.

"Those t-tights," I said, but the volume had gone out of my voice. I took a shuddering breath, and when I spoke again, the strength in my voice returned. "Take them off so I can see your real face."

She stopped spinning again and cocked that wretched head. "Mommy," she said. "This is my real face."

She slowly lifted her arm, finger pointing. On the chair in the corner of the room, splayed out as if it were made of melted wax with dead-alive eyes, was my Samantha's face. Blue eyes. Pink lips. Fair skin.

And hung on the back of the chair, like a golden silk scarf, was her long blonde hair.

Soul Eater

Betty Whalen's screams echo in the dark tunnel. She pulls and punches, trying to stop him from his task at hand.

Thomas Bain shoves Betty away from him, his other hand pinning her companion—a male with terror in his eyes—against the wall of the tunnel. There is blood on his neck. It pours over Thomas's hand. The heat of it stirs something inside him.

"No, please," Betty says. "I've changed my mind."

"It's too late for that, love, don't you think?" Thomas says.

Blood oozes down the sidewalk. A great flood of it. The terror in the man's eyes drifts away as he releases his last breath.

Now the best part. He has to catch it before it escapes. Thomas pulls the man's mouth open and shoves his hand inside, pushing farther until he is up to his elbow. He feels it.

The soul.

He tugs at it until it gives with a pop like a creaky joint. When it is out, it holds the shape of a heart. Not a

Valentine-I-Love-You heart. A real blood-pumping-life-giving heart. It holds that shape for a few seconds before falling into an amorphous lump in his palm.

Betty comes to him.

"That's it?" she asks. "All that for this thing?"

Thomas rolls his eyes. They are always disappointed. "What did you expect?"

"Something … else. Glowing maybe?"

The misshapen lump is gray, like a mound of clay.

"Take it," Thomas says. He shoves it her way. She holds out her hands. He drops it into her palms.

"What do I do?" she asks.

"Swallow it."

She lifts it to her lips—it's the size of a grapefruit—and tries to bite it.

"No, not like that. It doesn't work to bite it. Souls are tough and not easily separated into pieces. Hold it to your lips and slurp. It'll change."

She does. Slurps it right down. She gasps in a choke and grabs her throat.

"Oh, dear. I forgot to mention," Thomas says with a wide and wicked grin. "Not everyone can be a soul eater."

Tomoeba

We were on a deep-sea mission to discover new organisms. A team erected a submarine habitat on the side of the Mariana Trench at around 15,000 feet. A tiny sub took us down two at a time. Char is a semester away from becoming a marine biologist, though she may rethink her major now. I've been studying microbiology with a minor in ecology. Single-cell organisms and their impact on various ecosystems, including marine, have always fascinated me. Char and I were hand-selected by the head of the program because of our extraordinary contributions to science. Bullshit, if you ask me. I think they wanted private funding, and we both have wealthy parents. Don't get me wrong, we have headed up some significant research projects on our paths to our PhDs. We have clout. But money speaks much louder.

The advance team had been down there for three months when we joined them for our three-week stint in the darkest part of the ocean. The place where monsters lurk.

They'd already collected quite a few sediment and rock samples by the time Char and I got there. The team received us, at first, with about as much welcome as a leper to a hot tub party, but once they found out who we were, and what our parents contributed, they opened up.

Char got more attention because of her thesis, plus her intelligence and charisma demand attention. She isn't the most beautiful girl out there, but she can talk to anyone, no matter rank, role, or age. She just fits in. Anywhere and everywhere. That's what drew me to her in the first place. To this day, I don't know why she picked me as her girlfriend.

I felt like I was just a tagalong. I'm a little on the introverted side. Okay, a lot on the introverted side. Anxiety and all.

And I really hate water.

Anyway, I won't bore you with the minutia of meet and greets. We had all the right specialists on the advance team. The most important, to me, were Jessica Smith, a full-fledged marine biologist, Ignacio Stevens, in charge of dive operations, Penelope Rogers, our cook, and Tom Jacobs, a microbiologist, like me.

Tom always wandered around the hab whistling "Yellow Submarine." He winked at everyone but never said hello. He had an 80s porn-star mustache, and despite that, I liked him right away. He made me feel welcome and called Char, "Charlotte's Web," all the time, even though Char is short for Charlene. That's just Tom. When he found out I was studying microbiology, he took me to the dark lab.

The dark lab is through an airlock and down. It's just what it sounds like, really. A lab that is always dark. The only light is a red light in the doorway from the airlock.

When you go in, you put on night vision goggles so you can see what's kept in the tanks. Tom says it is to protect the specimens. They aren't used to light in their natural environment.

Microscopes fitted to the tanks scan the cubic volume of each rectangular holding bin since most of the samples from the bottom of the trench are single-cell organisms.

"We found sixty-eight new species of bacteria in the first sediment sample alone," he says with a twinkle in his eye. "And these." He moves to a tank holding a handful of weird, fat, shrimp-looking animals with translucent shells.

"All hands on deck," someone yells from above. Tom and I take off our goggles and climb up into the airlock. After disinfecting, we head to the main cabin.

Jessica has returned from her latest excursion in the weird, vertical sub James Cameron designed when he made history and was the first to explore at 27,000 feet.

"Happy birthday, Tom," Jessica says. She hands him a towel-wrapped parcel and kisses his cheek. "Should have seen how it reacted to the LEDs."

Tom grins at me and nods his head toward the ladder to the dark lab.

"We'll have to watch the mission recording to see what she's talking about," Tom says. "For now, we'll put this guy over here." He submerges the jar into an empty tank and unscrews the lid, then pulls his hands out slowly. I can just make out the creature in my night vision goggles.

The thing is shapeless and nearly invisible if not for the nucleus, which almost glows red.

"What is it?" I ask.

"This is the fun part," Tom says. "We get to name it." He strokes his mustache. "How about Tomoeba?"

I turn my head and catch his wide grin in my goggles.

.   .   .

Char has been spending a lot of time with Jessica. I have hardly seen her for the past three days.

Later that day, or night—hard to tell when you're under the ocean with metric tons of pressure all around—Tom and I watch the recording from Jessica's dive.

The recording has shots from various cameras from the sub. One of Jessica's port side lights reflects off something silver. Just a tiny flash. I'm not even sure how she saw it if she wasn't looking for it. When she moves the sub closer, the Tomoeba shifts and changes color like an oil slick. Murky greens and purples. It seems to writhe.

"Looks like it's in pain," I whisper. "The way it moves like that."

Tom grunts a reply. I'm not sure if he agrees with me or is just acknowledging I said something. Jessica turns off the light in the recording and switches to night vision. The Tomoeba mimics the shape of the sub and the shape of the arm that swings over to collect it.

"Eat your heart out, Tom," Jessica says on screen.

Tom covers the other tanks with black out cloth, then gets an LED flashlight from a drawer. He clicks it on and shines it on the Tomoeba. It reacts the same way as it did on the video, twisting and tumbling, rippling with color.

"Whoa," I say. I look at Tom, who was staring intently at the thing. The muscle in his jaw twitches and a smile forms on his lips. His eyes widen.

"Maybe you should stop now," I tell him. He keeps shining the light on the thing. "Tom, stop." I swear I can hear a faint scream coming from the tank. I shake his shoulder.

He turns his head and looks at me but keeps the light on the water. We hold each other's eyes for a few seconds until a *tink* comes from the tank.

The Tomoeba is gone. In its place is a ball about the size of a quarter sitting on the bottom. It looks like a pill bug all rolled up to protect itself.

Tom's swallow is audible in the quiet lab.

"What happened?" I ask. "How did it ... do that?"

Tom shakes his head, his eyes wide. "I've never seen anything like it." His voice is husky. He clears his throat. With the light off, the Tomoeba stays still and ball-like.

"Is it dead?" I ask in a whisper.

"It's like it evolved in a matter of seconds. Were you watching when it happened?" Tom asks, as if he hadn't been there holding my gaze just a minute ago.

I shake my head.

Later, after dinner, I find Char in our room and sit with her for what seems like the first time in days. She tells me about the things she is learning from Jessica. I tell her about the Tomoeba, and Tom.

"It was like he enjoyed hurting it, if the light actually hurt it," I tell her. "And then it changed. Like ... rapid evolution to protect itself from the light." I tell her how Tom seemed to forget what happened.

"He was just excited, I'm sure," Char says. "Isn't it great to be with people like us? People who geek out on the same things we do?" Her smile is infectious. I almost don't notice her change of subject. "Jessica said I can stay longer, if I want."

I look up from my *Walking Dead* graphic novel. "Are you going to?"

"I don't know," Char says. "I wanted to talk to you about it first."

The next sub to the surface was to arrive in two weeks

to take us back. After that, it would be another two months for a supply drop. I know I can survive without Char for that long, but a part of me is hurt she sprung it on me like this. Our joint project is due at the end of the quarter. It would give us only one month to wrap up our research and write our paper. She must sense my apprehension, because she crawls over to my bunk and lays her head on my stomach, then pulls my book down.

"It would be an amazing opportunity," I tell her, though my voice fails to inflect the excitement I should feel for her. Maybe I'm jealous Tom didn't ask me to stay. I've sort of just been his shadow in the lab these past few days. Char has actually been helping Jessica with research and dissections and documentation. Like an assistant. Participating, not just standing by watching.

"You don't mean that," Char says. She knows me too well.

"It's just, you know, our project. We need to finish it to get our final grade."

"We can take an incomplete and finish it later," she says.

"What about your thesis?"

"This will enhance my dissertation."

"What about our plans?" I sit up, and she rolls onto her butt on the floor by my bunk. I slide down next to her and lift her left hand.

The ring I got for her is one of those silicone bands in her favorite color, blue, like the ocean. I told her I'd get her something flashier, but she loves how functional it is. She doesn't have to worry about it getting dirty, or breaking it, or anything like that.

"We have a lifetime to figure that out," she says. She kisses my cheek, then my lips. I pull away, though.

"Don't coerce me," I tell her with a smile. She keeps kissing me. "This is entrapment," I say past her lips.

"Ahem," someone clears their throat in the doorway. Jessica. "Hey, Char," she says. "Can you help me for a minute?"

Char's face brightens. She gets up and follows Jessica out without a backward glance. I sigh.

I find Tom in the dark lab. He's hovering by the tank with the Tomoeba. He has an elbow propped on the top corner and he's gazing into the water. His other hand is resting on the edge, his index and middle fingers dangling below the surface. The Tomoeba is still rolled up in a ball.

"What are you calling it now that it has shape?" I ask him. He startles. "Oh, sorry," I laugh. "I thought you heard me come in."

"What do you want?" His voice is sharp around the edges. He doesn't look up from the tank. I stop walking toward him.

"Uh, nothing. Just thought you might want some help down here."

"I don't," he says. "You should go."

I turn to leave but pause. "I'm here to be your assistant," I tell him. "But all I do is follow you around. I'm supposed to be furthering my education. Teach me something, please?" My heart pounds in my ears. I'm only able to say this because it's dark in the lab. I'm hidden. He can't see how my face flushes, how sweat breaks out on my upper lip.

"You want to learn something?" He finally turns from the tank and steps toward me, one hand still in the water. "Learn to mind your own fu—" he releases the top edge. His face changes from anger to relaxed surprise. "Oh, hey Dana. I didn't hear you come in."

What the hell?

My hands are shaking from the encounter.

"What's going on?" he asks with a smile. "Everything okay?" He takes off his goggles and wipes his brow. "Man, is it hot in here, or what?" I've never heard Tom string so many words together.

"I was just … going to ask you what you're calling it now that it has a shape."

He shrugs. "Not sure yet," he says. "We can keep calling it the Tomoeba. Do you want to call it that?"

"I don't think it's up to me," I say. I keep backing away from him as he comes closer.

"Sure it is. You're my student, right?" His smile is plastered in place.

"I think Tomoeba is fine," I say. "I should get to bed." I climb up when Tom grabs my ankle. I let out a short shriek.

"You can't take those out of here," he says, pointing at my face. I pull the goggles off and hand them to him. He holds onto my ankle for a few seconds too long, then lets go. "I'm doing some experiments on the Tomoeba tomorrow," he says. "I'd like you to assist me."

"Okay," I say, then climb up and head to my bunk. Char isn't there. I need her to be here after what just happened with Tom. I pace the room for a few minutes, then lay on my bunk with my book.

Next thing I know, it's morning, at least I think it's morning. Char is gone or was never here. Her bunk is perfectly made as if she hadn't slept in it. I get up, brush my teeth, and make my way to the kitchen for a bite to eat. Everyone is there, bright-eyed and ready to tackle another day in the great deep. Everyone except Tom.

"Morning, sleepyhead." Char plants a kiss on my cheek then spins out of the room after Jessica. I grab for her hand, but she's too quick.

"Hey," I say, sitting down at a table full of people I don't really know that well. Aside from Penny, the cook. She scowls at me.

"Food ain't gonna serve itself," she says from the stove.

"I know, I know," I say. "Coffee, then food." I shuffle to the coffee pot, but it's empty.

"Gotta get up earlier than that to get some brew," Penny says. I sigh. Why didn't Char get me up to eat breakfast with her?

I shuffle out of the kitchen to the dark lab. The lab is quiet, except for the ambient noises of a submarine habitat at 15,000 feet under the ocean. Don't think about that. I step off the ladder into a puddle of water, grab a pair of goggles, and flip them on. I stifle a scream at the last nanosecond.

Tom is at the Tomoeba tank. Maybe he never left. The other tanks, the ones with sediment and rock samples, and unknown bacteria in them, are smashed to pieces. Water covers the floor. What if one or more of the sixty-eight bacteria are deadly? I turn quick and grab a mask, though if they survive in the air and are airborne, it's too late.

"Tom?" I say from the bottom of the ladder. My voice catches. "Tom? What happened in here?"

He doesn't move. I know he's alive because he's standing, and because his two fingers are in the tank, moving slightly, and because I can hear his rasping breaths. I grab another ventilator and strap it on his face. He doesn't seem to notice. The Tomoeba tank looks empty.

"Tom?" When I say it this time, it is a whisper. I clear my throat and say his name again, with authority.

He looks up, slowly.

"I had a dream last night," he says. "A dream about you and me." His voice is dreamy and high. "We were lovers."

"Why are you telling me this?" My voice goes an octave too high. "It's just going to make things weird."

"Things are already weird, Georgia," he says. Georgia? Who the fuck is Georgia? "I never stopped loving you." He turns far enough that his hand comes out of the water, but, unlike last time, his face remains … weird. Vacant eyes seeming to look at nothing.

"Where is the Tomoeba?" I ask, backing away toward the ladder.

"There never was another woman I loved more than you," he says, reaching for me. I get to the ladder and up before he even reaches the bottom. I pull off the goggles and scramble out into the airlock, slamming and locking it behind me. I disinfect and get out of there.

"Dana?" Ignacio is behind me. "Everything all right little sis?" He calls all the girls little sis because he has seven sisters all younger than him.

"Something's wrong with Tom," I say. "He smashed all the tanks, and he's talking about someone named Georgia."

Ignacio laughs, but it sounds nervous. "Tom's such a joker." He ignores what I feel is a look of panic and fear on my face and shakes his head while wandering off down the hall.

Tom hits the window on the airlock behind me. I whirl around. Since I locked it from the outside, he can't get out.

"Dana," his mouth says. He pushes the intercom button and says my name again. "Come on, is this some kind of joke? Who broke the tanks?"

I push the button on my side and tell him, "You did."

His face is one of disbelief.

"Where is the Tomoeba, Tom?" I ask him. "It wasn't in the tank."

He smiles then, and his lips stretch wide. His mouth

opens and the top of his head flips back like in those old Reach toothbrush commercials from the 90s. *You can either get a flip-top head …*

A pair of translucent antennae poke out of the opening, twitching around. Each has a black spot at the top. It presses the black spots against the glass, leaving greasy tracks, like slug slime. They twitch back and forth and seem to land on my face, on my eyes.

I cry out and back away, then scramble down the hall after Ignacio, hoping to find someone who will believe what happened.

"Someone help!" I shout.

Jessica and Char step into the hall, chatting excitedly.

"Char!" I call. She doesn't turn around. "Jessica?" No response. I know they can hear me. This whole fucking place is a giant metal cone. Everything echoes. It's maddening sometimes.

They can't hear you. It's a male voice, Tom's voice, but slightly different. Muffled with a liquid quality. I turn around and gape toward the airlock.

His face is in the window. His normal, regular face. Not the hyperextended jaw with the creature emerging. I slowly walk back toward him.

"What do you mean?" I ask.

"They can't hear you, Georgia," Tom says, his mouth hardly moving, as if he were doing ventriloquism.

"Why are you calling me Georgia?" I ask. "Why can't they hear me?"

You don't exist. His voice is a gurgly whisper in my mind. He backs away from the window into the dark, and I run away to find Char and Jessica and anyone else.

I find Char in our room and envelope her in my arms so tightly she grunts and wraps hers around me in return. My body shakes with sobs.

"What's going on?" she asks.

"Tom … the thing Jessica brought back … I don't know what's going on." I get the words out through choked sobbing and sniffling. Char pulls away and looks at me, wipes away my tears.

"Slow down," she says in a soothing voice. "What happened with Tom?"

I look into her big blue eyes, wide with concern, and as I tell her what happened, it sounds so ridiculous, I can't even believe it happened.

Before I get to tell her about Tom's flip-top head, Tom appears in the doorway.

"Knock knock, ladies," he says, a grin stretched across his face.

"Tom." I gasp his name and take a step back, gripping Char's wrist in case I need to pull her behind me … or in front of me. I search his face for any signs of his mouth being ripped open.

"I didn't mean to frighten you, Dana," he says, putting emphasis on my name as if to show he knows I'm not Georgia. Char gently pulls her wrist out of my grasp. I can't help but notice the strange look she gives me out of the corner of my eye. It's one part who-are-you-even and one part annoyance.

"I could use your help," Tom says. "In the dark lab."

I gulp. His eyes twinkle. I stupidly nod. "Okay." The word comes out thick through the dryness in my throat. "Can Char come, too? I want her to see the… Tomoeba."

Tom looks at Char. "Charlotte's Web is welcome anytime. If she wants to come. Do you want to come?" His eyes flick to her. They widen.

"No, I think Jessica needs my help," Char says in a monotone voice.

"Char, please?" I whisper to her. "I really want to show you."

She doesn't look at me. Just walks away like I didn't even ask her.

Tom rubs his hands together and jerks his head toward the hallway. "Come on then, assistant." He says the last word with a French accent.

I follow him to the airlock. There is no sign the thing had pressed its eyestalks against the glass. No smears or anything. He must have cleaned them off before coming out to find me.

We climb down into the lab. The glass from the broken tanks sits in a pile in one corner with the dustpan next to it.

"What happened to the tanks?" Inside, my heart thunders against my ribcage, threatening to break out. I was sure he could hear it. I sweat inside my protective suit.

"The Tomoeba smashed them, Dana," Tom says matter-of-factly.

It could be true. I didn't actually witness him smashing them. But the fact that he was still in the lab afterward, as if nothing had happened, still touching the Tomoeba tank with his fingers drifting beneath the surface had made me think differently.

"It evolved again, Dana. It grew appendages … long appendages that unfurled from that little armored body." His eyes sparkle in the red glow of the lights. His voice has softened but also raised an octave and a half. His lips hold a grin.

I shift my eyes to the Tomoeba tank where a creature swims back and forth. Octopus-like arms furl and unfurl as it swims as if testing the boundaries of the glass. Without thinking, I move closer.

"Holy shit," I whisper. He wasn't lying. I feel instantly

safer, but also confused. What the hell did I see then? Was it my imagination? A nightmare?

"It's incredible, Dana," Tom says. "I've never seen anything like it."

"What does it mean?" I ask.

Tom shakes his head and leans over to peer through the glass. "I don't know. I just don't know, Dana."

He keeps using my name. It's unnerving and unnatural.

"This kind of rapid evolution is unheard of, Dana." He paces away from the tank. "The thing is adapting to its surroundings. First forming a protective barrier around itself, and now growing these arms to move around faster, easier."

"Tom," Jessica's voice breaks through the overhead speakers. We both look up as if she's floating in the corner. "I got another one."

Tom looks at me, eyes too wide. "Excellent." He rushes up the ladder.

A week goes by. Tom and I observe the new creature which we didn't torture with a flashlight, and the first one, the Tomoeba. Tom puts them in side-by-side tanks, the only two creatures in the lab now, in the only two aquariums.

The Tomoeba spends a lot of time at the far end of its enclosure, seeming to look in at the other one. Tom put a lid on the tank because it kept reaching tentacles over. They weren't long enough to do any damage, but he told me he figured the thing would probably evolve to make them longer. He says he fears they might be territorial. But we would never know.

Before we can learn much more from them, Tom dissects one. He brought the idea up when I was in the lab once, and I told him it was a bad idea. I thought he agreed with me, but a few days later, I enter the lab and there he is, with the Tomoeba outside of the tank, stretched out on a table. It is the size of a large cuttlefish now—about twenty inches long.

Tom slides the scalpel down the length of its body.

"Tom, no," I shout. I trip on the ladder and face plant onto the floor. Tom turns around, a wide grin on his face.

"We need to see what makes it tick, Georgia," he says.

Oh shit.

He removes his mask.

I reach for him, yelling for him to stop. He lashes out with the scalpel, nicking my gloved hand. I recoil and check the cut. Blood oozes from it.

We don't know if the creatures from the deep are toxic or not. I look up just as Tom slides the scalpel across his own throat, laughing at first a throaty laugh, then a gurgled one that's cut short as he flops to the floor.

I scream and clamber up the ladder. Shouting for Char, Jessica, Ignacio, anyone.

I run to our room, still in my dark lab gear. Char and Jessica are both there, sitting close together, bent over a book Char had brought. Shoulder to shoulder.

They look up at me, smiling at first, then confusion replaces their grins.

"Tom just killed himself," I shout through tears.

"Dana," Jessica says. "Did you decompress in the airlock before wearing that out here?"

"No," I yell. "Tom needs help."

"You know the rules," Char says. "You could be contaminated."

"Didn't you hear what I said?" I yell, coming closer. They both recoil from me, shrinking away like I'm covered in bacteria or infested with bugs. "Tom … he cut his own throat."

"Dana," a voice behind me says. I whirl around. Tom is there, frowning. "You left right when I needed your help."

I back away from him.

"Are you feeling okay, Dana?" Char asks, but she doesn't come closer. She and Jessica cling to each other at the back of our room. Isn't that just cute?

I don't know what to do or say, so I laugh. I laugh because if I don't, I might burst into tears.

"J-just kidding," I say. "It was a joke." But I look at my hand where Tom's blade slit my glove. Where dried blood crusts the hole.

Later, alone with Char, I tell her I need to go back to the surface. We are sitting on the floor in our room, cross-legged, facing each other.

"Underwater life is not for me," I tell her. She opens her mouth to protest, but I hold up my hand. "You can stay. I know this is a huge opportunity for you. Stay for the whole summer. Study with Jessica. But I want you to be honest with me before I go."

She swallows hard and nods. "I'm always honest with you," she says.

I look down and clasp her hands. "I don't know how to ask this without sounding psycho … so I'll just ask." I meet her eyes. "Is there something going on between you and Jessica?"

Char shakes her head. "Not at all. She has a husband up top."

I feel the relief rush into my body.

"She's just taken me under her wing," Char keeps talking. "She's more like a mother than anything else."

I lean forward and hug her. "I'm sorry I can't stay here."

"Don't be sorry, Dana," she says. "I knew from the beginning, with your claustrophobia, this might not work out."

Even though I know she's talking about living on the side of the Mariana Trench, I still feel a pang in my heart at her last five words.

This might not work out.

I have thought those words in the past, before I asked her to marry me, in the early stages of our relationship. She's a severe extrovert, and I could live in a cave alone my entire life.

"I'll let the team know tomorrow," I say.

We sleep in the same tiny bunk and give each other a proper goodbye.

I'm awakened by hollow thumping sounds. I open my eyes. Char is wrapped around me like a squid. All arms and legs tangled in mine. I extract myself from her embrace.

Another *thump* followed by a male's cry. I pull on my discarded clothes and crack open the door.

Smashing glass sounds from down the hall, followed by another shout.

I rush down the hall. The airlock to the dark lab is open. I don't bother with a suit. If there are harmful bacteria in there, they're out now.

I take the ladder the fast way, sliding down the handrails, and land with a splash at the bottom.

In the glow of the red light, Tom is on the floor. His chest heaves with shallow, rapid breaths. Blood spills down the front of his shirt from his mouth. I crouch by his side, back against the wall.

"Tom," I whisper as I look around the lab.

Water spills out of the smashed Tomoeba tank, pooling on the floor. I don't see the creature anywhere.

"It got them," Tom says. "It got them all, Georgia. They're all dead." He swallows hard.

"Who?"

"The crew," he says, anguish painting his voice. "Jessica, Ignacio, Penny, all of them."

"Where is it now?" I ask him.

"It can breathe air," he says. "It's evolved again."

"Where is it, Tom?"

"I don't—I don't know."

I grab the scalpel off the tray Tom had used earlier when I thought I saw him dissecting the thing. I need to get back to our room and get Char out of here before the Tomoeba finds her and kills her, too. I climb out of the dark lab and run down the hall. Something wraps around my ankle. I trip, almost landing on the scalpel.

Runs with scissors goes through my mind.

Something squeezes my ankle. I look down. A translucent tentacle grips my leg, undulating as it squeezes tighter. The suction cups burn my skin. I scream and lash out with the scalpel, slicing into the flesh. Blue spurts out, and the thing screams from somewhere down the hall. The tentacle recoils, slithering backward in a flopping back and forth movement, pinballing off the walls. I scramble to my feet.

"Char, Char," I yell as I bust into our room, the heavy metal door clanging against the side of her bunk. She's sitting upright, groggy as hell.

"What is it?" she asks in a sleep-filled voice. I grab her arm.

"We have to go," I pull her to her feet and throw her clothes at her. "Put those on, quick." I can't stop the panic from entering my voice. She's moving too slow. I help her with her pants, holding them open for her like she's a toddler. She steps into them and pulls on her shirt. I grab her wrist and drag her down the hall toward the minisub. Jessica gave us a tutorial on how to drive it when we first arrived. I prayed to anything holy that I remembered, and that learning by watching would serve me.

We pull on dry suits.

"What's going on, Dana?" Char asks me, fully awake now that I have her by the escape subs.

"The Tomoeba," I say. "It killed everyone."

"Jessica," Char says in a gasping whisper. She turns around, but I whirl her back roughly by the shoulder.

"She's dead, Char. They all are." I push her into the sub. "We have to get out of here." I've held it together so far. Char's wide eyes and trembling lip almost break me.

The Tomoeba slithers into view. It is horrifying. Sloppy gooey skin with the faces of everyone morphing out of the side of it. Tom's face is in the front between the thing's massive eyestalks. Tentacles lash out toward the door, but I slam it and crank the airlock.

Char is crying behind me, barely contained screams drowned by snot and tears.

As we pull away in the minisub and head toward the surface, I try not to think about how far we have to go, how many miles of water are above us, what lurks below. At one point, I see a tentacle reaching out of the side window, but it proves to be a school of fish. We are leaving the deep.

The rest of the trip to the surface is a blur of endless dark, Char's sobs, and my heavy breathing. I can't seem to get enough air in my lungs.

The next thing I know, Char and I are on the beach on

our knees clutching each other, staring toward the waves. The thick dry suits we wore during our escape are piled on the ground nearby, shed after we reached the surface in the minisub and swam to shore over an hour ago. We've been staring at the Pacific Ocean ever since, waiting for the *thing* to rise to the surface. I know it will eventually. I know it will come for us.

"What was it?" Char asks. "Dana, what was it?"

She's been sobbing quietly since we made it to shore and hasn't loosened her trembling grip on my arm. I still don't even know how we got away. Alive. The *thing* advanced so fast.

"Didn't you see it?" I ask her. She looks at me with wide eyes, takes a deep breath, and shakes her head.

"I ran because you did. Because of the panic a-a-and fear in your voice."

I thought she saw it. I look out over the lapping waves illuminated by moonlight and wonder if I really saw what I saw.

After doing some research, I found out Georgia was Tom's assistant who died during an exploration. A picture of her shows—if I squint my eyes—a woman who looks like me. Same hair color, face shape, eye color. Same overall appearance, really, like she could be my aunt or something.

Char hasn't been the same since we escaped. Cold and distant. Every morning she checks various news sites looking for information from the Trench. One morning, two weeks post-escape, they finally come.

I was wrong. Everyone is still alive.

"Dana," Char says in a low and even tone. I look up from my bowl of cereal and meet her gaze. Her cheeks are flushed, and her lips are set in a tight line. "Look at this." She pushes her iPad across the table.

The second I lower my eyes to the screen a bomb drops into my gut. I read the article. Not only are they alive and well, but the crew has found more organisms, more bacteria, more micro-environments, more … everything. The article speaks of awards the team will get, recognition, esteem. All things Char wanted. All things I took from her when we left.

"Is it because of Jessica?" she asks in that calm, angry tone I've only been on the receiving end of once in our relationship. I can't meet her eyes.

"I'm sorry." My voice is a strangled sound.

"You ruined my chances," she starts. Her voice breaks off with a sob. She collects herself. "You ruined my chances of being *anything* in my field." She's at a point of lividness that I will never understand. Usually eloquent and never at a loss for words, her lips press together and her nostrils flare. There are tears in her eyes, but they don't fall.

I don't stop her when she packs up the items she keeps at my place, and I don't stop her when she leaves her key on the table.

I don't know what happened down there, but I am doing all I can to figure it out. Hallucinations from claustrophobia? Is that a thing? My therapist says anything is possible.

After an emotional session, I go home and get ready for an early bedtime. I lean over the sink and splash water on my face and drink cupped palmful after cupped palmful.

A tickle in my throat sends me into a coughing fit. There's something in there. Something in my throat. I suddenly can't breathe.

I stand upright and open my mouth wide, wheezing as air barely moves past the blockage. I reach in and hook my finger around something thin and slimy. I pull, but it's too slick. I open my mouth wider and fumble with my phone to turn on the flashlight, a panicked squeak squeezing out of my throat. I point the light at my mouth and stick my tongue out as far as I can.

At the back of my mouth, tickling my uvula, is a semitranslucent eyestalk. The little black spot in the center of it meets my eye in the mirror.

Sometimes He Laughs

The room at the top of the stairs didn't exist. Someone wallpapered over it, and it didn't show up on the blueprints, either. As if whoever revised the records didn't want anyone to know it was there. Someone stole the original blueprints over a hundred years ago. My dad said so when he came back from the records office. He and Mom were in the kitchen talking about it.

"Funny thing is," Dad said. "From the outside, there can't possibly be a room." He scratched his head and shrugged. "But why else would there be stairs?"

"Let's check it out," Mom said. She loved a good mystery.

I was outside the kitchen doorway, peeking inside. I was with Mom on this one. I'd gone up there every day, wondering what was beyond the horrid floral wallpaper. Touching the wall, feeling for seams. I could tell the wall behind the paper was not smooth.

I backed away from the kitchen when I heard Mom's chair scrape the floor, and their two sets of footsteps coming toward me. Mom appeared first.

"We're going to take a look, Sally," Mom said. She knew I'd been listening. Her eyes twinkled at me. "Go find your brother."

She liked to discover things as a family. I found Chad playing in his room.

"Dad's gonna open it up," I said to Chad, pointing to the ceiling. He was only three but knew what I meant. He scrambled to his feet, clutching a Hot Wheels car in his chubby fist. I took his other hand, and we met our mom and dad at the bottom of the stairs.

Dad clicked on a flashlight and held it under his chin. "Here we go," he said in a spooky voice.

I giggled, but Chad cringed and tucked himself behind me a little, his hand squeezing mine. Mom smoothed his fine blonde hair away from his forehead.

"It's okay, baby," she said. He grinned at her and his grip on my hand loosened and he reached for our mom. She lifted him into her arms and bounced him around.

"Shall we?" Dad climbed the stairs. We piled in behind him. He shined the light on the wall at the top.

"There aren't any seams," I told him in my authoritative voice. "I've checked."

Dad pulled his pocketknife out of his jeans and flicked the blade open. He felt along the wall and made several poking holes in the paper, then started tearing it away. When he'd done enough, he pointed the flashlight at the remains of sticky glue and torn paper fragments.

"Interesting," he said.

"What is?" I asked.

"Whoever walled this up was in a hurry."

Dad knew construction because he'd built lots of houses and prided himself in his masonry, as he called it. I called it brickwork because I could never remember the word for it.

I stood on my tippy toes and tried to look over and around mom. She turned sideways so I could see. It was a stone wall. The cracks filled in with sloppy amounts of mortar. Even I could tell it wasn't done properly.

"I need more tools," Dad said.

"More tools," Chad mimicked. He toyed with Mom's hair. "Hungry, hungry, hungry."

"Okay, little snacker." Mom rubbed her nose against his, then lifted her eyes to Dad. "Be sure to seal off the entry to minimize the dust, Love." Mom used her sing-song voice and squeezed past me down the stairs. Dad and I stayed by the wall.

"Wanna help me, Littles?" he asked me.

I nodded vigorously. I loved to help Dad do things. Ever since Chad came around, Mom's attention had been preoccupied with raising him, but Dad seemed to realize that I still needed attention, too. He always asked me if I wanted to help, and I always said yes.

We got the supplies we needed from the shed out back and got to work. Dad did most of it, but I held the light so he could see. We both wore masks that covered our noses and mouths, earplugs to protect our hearing, and goggles to keep our eyes in our heads. It was fun to see Dad smash the stones, and how easy it looked. He asked me if I wanted to try, and I could hardly lift the mallet, so he helped me swing it, and we knocked a big stone out of the wall. It tumbled down the stairs, which we'd covered in thick blankets to protect the wood.

"Good job," Dad said. He gave me a high five.

When Dad finished smashing the wall down, there was a black door behind it. I wanted to see what was inside before anyone else. I wanted to be the first one, but Dad told me to go get Mom, and getting Mom meant getting Chad.

"Can we look before anyone else, please?" I asked. "Please?" I pitched my voice higher to the cherries-on-top level.

Dad laughed. "How can I resist that tone and those eyes?" He pinched my nose. "Don't tell Mom and Chad." He took the flashlight from my grip and on the count of three opened the door. He shined the light around, lingering in the doorway. I bounced back and forth from foot to foot, eager to see what was on the other side, but he blocked my view. A light came on around him, and he clicked the flashlight off. The bulb in the middle of the ceiling flickered and buzzed. Dad put his hand on the switch. The light evened out, and Dad let out a breath.

"Lemme see, lemme see!"

Dad stepped inside. I followed.

There wasn't much. A big room with doors along the walls. Little doors, like cupboards. I ran toward the first one, but Dad grabbed my shoulder, halting me in my tracks.

"Hold on," he said, crouching down to my level and wrapping an arm around my back. "I think I should check the doors first. Go on downstairs with your mom and Chad."

I shook my head. "No way, Jose. I want to see what's in there."

"There're probably spiders and rats in there."

A creepy-crawly feeling skittered up my back, and I shrieked. Dad wiggled his fingers in front of me. I laughed.

"Seriously, though, kiddo," he said, this time in his definite serious voice. "Go on. I'll check it out first, then you can come up and see."

"Before Chad?"

He nodded. "Yep. Before Chad."

"Tom?" Mom yelled up the stairs. Her voice was full of alarm. Her feet pounded on the wooden steps. "Tom."

Mom had a paper towel around her hand. It was bright red. Droplets dripped onto the floor.

"Jesus, Holly, what happened?" Dad rushed to Mom. He peeled back the paper towel. "Holy shit. This needs stitches."

"I was cutting a tomato with that super sharp knife," she said in a breathless voice that frightened me. "Chad was on the floor and I turned to look—he was about to stick a fork in the socket by the kitchen cart." She made a slicing motion with her hand. "Slipped."

Dad turned to me. "Sally," he said in a low voice. "I need you to watch your brother while I take Mom to the emergency room."

I didn't look at his eyes or his face. I was too fixated on Mom's hand and the blood that was *drip-drip-dripping* from her makeshift bandage.

"I'm not old enough," I told him, even though a week ago I told them I *was* old enough to watch him while they went to the grocery store. I hadn't wanted to go, but they told me I was too young to stay home alone.

"Just this once. We won't be long." Dad gripped my forearms. "Take Chad to his room and you two play there until we get home, okay?" I met his eyes this time. The patter of Mom's blood dripping loud in my ears.

"Okay," I said. I knew it was important for him to get her to the doctor. So much blood. The paper towel was red and so soaking wet it wasn't holding any more fluid.

I followed them down the stairs and found Chad in the living room. Stupid brother. He was old enough to know better than to stick a fork in a socket. A nasty part of me— the little devil, Mom called it—wished he had. It was a bad thought, I know, but ever since Chad came around everything was too different.

I took his hand.

"Mommy and Daddy are going to the doctor," I told him. "Let's play in your room until they get back." With all his stupid baby toys. He grinned at me.

"Okay, Sally." His 'L' sounds came out as 'W' sounds.

We went up the stairs. I helped him. He could do stairs on his own, but it would take twice as long. We went into his room, and he plopped on the floor and started playing with the nearest toys.

I sat with him and we played Crash Cars for a little while which was just slamming two rolling toys against each other as hard as we could. Usually, this game ended with someone getting a finger in the way and tears.

I wanted to go up to the room with all the doors. I wanted to see what was inside. Dad left the flashlight up there. I casually got up and started piling toys, making a moat of them around Chad.

If I hurried, I could get up there, check it out, and come back before Chad even got through the first layer of toys to follow me. If I closed the door behind me, it would give me another few seconds.

"Be right back," I said, patting him on the top of his head.

"Where going?" he asked in his annoying toddler broken English.

"To the bathroom," I lied.

"Poop?" He laughed.

"You're not supposed to say that, Little Devil."

He grinned and laughed again, then turned to the circle of cars I arranged around him. The second layer was bigger toys, then bigger ones, and finally a circle of stuffed animals, some of which used to be mine, but I generously gave them to him.

I slipped out the door while he busily made crashing sounds and drove two cars into each other. I hurried down the hall to the staircase and whipped aside the plastic curtain Dad set up to minimize the dust. I ran up, light-footed, barely making a sound in case Chad might hear I wasn't going to the bathroom. At the top, I found Dad's flashlight and flicked it on.

I shined it on the wall and found the light switch. I probably shouldn't flick it, but I didn't like having just a spot of light, so I didn't heed my own inner warning. I flicked it and the single bulb came on with the flicker and buzz like before. But this time it also snapped and popped and there were sparks and I almost screamed, but I slammed the switch back down and backed away from it.

The flashlight would have to do.

It was creepy up there. Dark and quiet. The little doors lining the walls called to me. They wanted me to peek inside.

I went to the first one and opened it. There was only darkness, and when I shined the light inside, the darkness went on for ages. I went around the room, and all the doors held the same thing.

I was just closing the last door on the left when I heard one of the other ones open. I whipped around just in time to see Chad disappear inside.

"Chad! No!" I screamed. He giggled in the darkness, but when I reached the door, he wasn't in there. At least, he wasn't close enough for the flashlight to hit him.

"Boo," I heard behind me. I turned around winging the circle of light around until it landed on his little face. He had popped out of a different door. He squealed in delight at my loud gasp, tossing his head back in glee.

Before I could stop him, he ducked back into the dark of that cabinet. I expected him to come out of the one I was still in front of, but he didn't. He came out of yet another one.

"How are you doing that?" I asked. I peered into the cupboard in front of me, but it was too dark, and I was old enough to know about fear of the dark. Chad wasn't. He was too stupid to know to be afraid.

He kept going in and popping out of other doors. Each time I wildly swung the light around, looking for him. It frightened me in that panicky way, like when Dad tickled me too much, and I didn't know if I should keep laughing or start crying. I chose laughter, but it was an uneasy sound. I wanted Chad to stop, but he was like the Whack A Prairie Dog at that dumb pizza place we went to one time. I didn't know which door he would pop out of next. The lack of light made it even worse.

I could hear his giggling even when the doors were closed.

And then I heard him scream.

"Chad? Chad?" I shrieked into the closest door. He cried the big hot cry of someone scared or hurt. "Chad! I'm coming to get you."

But I couldn't go in. It was too dark, and even though I made fun of Chad for having a night light, I now realized he didn't need, I slept with one, too. Because I actually needed one.

His crying kept going.

"Chad, it's okay!"

"Maaaaaaammmmeeeeee," he bawled.

Mom would be so mad. Dad would be mad. I had to go get him. I ran downstairs to the living room and grabbed a ball of yarn from Mom's knitting basket, though she'd stopped knitting when Chad was born. I ran back up the stairs and tied the end of the yarn to the knob on the door Chad first went into and held the ball in my hand.

"You can do this, Sally." I took a deep breath. "Here I come!" I called to him. I unwound the yarn as I went, shining the light straight ahead. In a second, there was another door. I went inside and popped out like Chad had. I wound the yarn around that doorknob and ducked back in. I hurried. Running through the short bursts of darkness inside those cupboards and back out into the not as dark room.

In a few minutes, I'd been through all the doors and hadn't found Chad.

He still cried. I joined him.

Mom and Dad found me up there, curled on the floor, wrapped around the ball of yarn.

"What's this about?" Dad asked with a smile, but he saw my face, which was probably blotchy and streaked with tears. Chad was still crying.

"Where's Chad?" Mom asked. Her hand was in a big white bandage. "Sally, where's Chad, honey?"

I burst into tears. "I don't know." The words bawled out of my throat like a roar.

Mom hurried around the room, touching the yarn on the knobs. Dad yelled for Chad into some of the dark interiors. Dad even followed my example and took the yarn and ran in and out of the doors. Mom screamed each time he popped out a different one. When Dad had been through them all, Mom tried. Screaming and shrieking Chad's name as he called to her in his wailing little voice.

. . .

They never found him. To this day, if anyone ever goes up to that non-existent third floor, they can still hear him crying.

But sometimes he laughs.

The Doll in the Corner

The Airbnb they found in the mountains didn't have any reviews yet, but it was cheap, and the pictures of the interior and surrounding property looked amazing. Trish and Pat booked it for their mountain getaway. It was their first anniversary.

Some people said the first year was the hardest. Adapting, getting to know each other on a different level, learning their habits and accepting them, or at least figuring out how to live with them. The problem was, though the first year had been smooth, Trish noticed changes in Pat she wasn't sure she liked. Subtle changes in the way he teased her, from flirty and fun when they'd first started dating, to almost bullying in the past month or two. He always waved it off if she didn't like it.

"I'm just teasing you. What happened to your sense of humor?"

.   .   .

They arrived at the vacation rental. Pat carried Trish's suitcase in and put it in the master bedroom on the ground floor.

Trish went upstairs and marveled at the place. The upper floor hosted an open floor plan—living room became dining room became kitchen. There was a bathroom right at the top of the stairs. It was a strange floor plan, but she liked the openness of it, and that there was a second, though smaller, bathroom upstairs. The stairs themselves were steep and narrow. The less they had to navigate them, the better.

"It's perfect, Pat," she said. "Look at this view." The living room on the upper level had a broad picture window that looked out at the Royal Mountains. King mountain towered over the rest, capped with snow down to the tree line, despite it being summer. "Does it always have snow?" she asked.

Pat had lived in the area before he met Trish. She looked to him as her local expert.

"All year round." He put his arm around her. She lifted her chin and kissed his jaw.

The owner appointed the house in a cute Scandinavian style. The only thing that seemed out of place among the clean lines and modern edge was a doll sitting on top of a wooden armoire in the living room.

He was dingy and wore a cap, like a strange version of Santa Claus dressed as a miner. He had a tiny pickaxe. His eyes were kind, and his nose and cheeks—the latter just visible through his beard—were rosy and lifted in a smile she couldn't see under all that hair.

"I can't tell if he's cute or kind of creepy," Trish said, pointing at the doll.

Pat stiffened. "I didn't even see him there." He moved toward the cabinet and poked the doll on the nose. It wobbled but didn't fall. "We should give him a name."

Trish laughed, but the sound was uneasy. "How about, no."

"I'm going to unload the rest of our stuff."

Trish unpacked their bags while Pat hauled the cooler upstairs and unloaded the essentials they'd brought with them. Mainly leftovers from their fridge at home, some olive oil, salt, and pepper.

That night, Trish had to use the bathroom. She didn't want to disturb Pat and was embarrassed since it was a number two. They hadn't reached the point in their marriage yet where she was comfortable with bathroom stuff. He could pee in front of her, but she liked her privacy. She decided to use the bathroom upstairs.

Trish slowly and carefully navigated the narrow staircase, gripping the railing as she climbed upward in darkness. At the top, she looked toward the window where scant amounts of moonlight filtered in.

The black form of the doll on top of the cabinet caught her eye.

"You better still be there when I come out," she said jokingly. But the thought frightened her. What if he wasn't there? She slipped into the bathroom and considered leaving the door open so she could keep an eye on him, but that freaked her out, too. She didn't want that doll to "see" her using the toilet.

After she finished, she opened the door and turned off the light and paused at the top of the stairs.

Don't look. Don't even look and you won't know.

She couldn't not look. She couldn't look. But she had to look. She lifted her eyes from the dark lower level to the picture window to the cabinet.

The corner was empty.

Trish let out a little squeaking scream and scrambled to turn on all the lights. It wasn't her home, though, and she couldn't remember where the light switches were.

She somehow got them all on.

"Trish?" Pat called from downstairs in a sleepy voice. "What are you doing up there, dancing?"

She opened her mouth to yell down to Pat but stopped. There was the doll, laying on the floor in front of the cabinet face down.

"Sorry, love," she called, moving around the sofa to the doll. She didn't want to touch it or see its face. She put a blanket over it, opened the cabinet, and stuffed it inside. She immediately felt better without his beady eyes staring out into the room.

The next morning, when Pat asked about the doll, she told him what happened. To her dismay, Pat laughed at her.

"Don't be silly, hun," he said. "It's an inanimate object. It's not going to come alive and get you in your sleep."

He was being kind of jerky. Trish ignored him until she heard the creak of the cabinet open. Pat pulled the blanket out, and when he shook it out, the doll was gone.

Trish jumped out of her chair. "It's gone? It's gone?" she asked, unable to keep the hysteria out of her voice.

Pat looked at her with wide eyes. "It's not in the blanket," he said.

Trish backed away from the table into the kitchen, and when her back hit the counter she gripped it. Unable to speak.

"Just kidding," Pat said. He produced the doll from the cabinet. "I took it out before I fluffed the blanket." He laughed. A cold, harsh sound.

"You're an asshole!" Trish shouted in a wavering voice.

"How could you be so mean?" Tears spilled down her cheeks.

"It was a joke," Pat said. "Jeeze, Trish, I'm sorry." He didn't sound sorry. There was still a jovial light shining in his eyes. He put the doll on top of the cabinet.

"Put it inside." She pointed at him, at the doll. "I don't want to see it."

Pat did as she told. His mouth turned down at the corners. He looked a little sheepish.

"I didn't realize," he said. "I'm sorry, really." He came to her and hugged her. Trish kept her eyes on the closed cabinet over his shoulder.

After a day of hiking and being outside in the mountain air, they had dinner and beers on the balcony. Pat had a few too many and passed out in bed without brushing his teeth. Trish crashed hard, too. But something woke her in the night, dragging her from those deep, deep levels of sleep and shoving her into the wakeful world.

It was a scratching sound. A *scraaaape, scraaaape*. She listened hard, holding her breath to add more silence.

Scraaaape. Scraaaape.

"Pat." She nudged him. "Pat, I hear a sound."

He grumbled something unintelligible and rolled over. Soft snores issued from his mouth. Trish frowned, irritated.

"Fine. I'll see what it is and get killed in the middle of the night." She flipped back the covers and made a show of getting out of bed, jostling so the headboard hit the wall as she flopped off the edge. She didn't creep but stomped. She didn't ease the door open but jerked it and let it hit the wall. Pat still slept.

She would dump the rest of his beer down the drain.

As she climbed the stairs, listening for the sound, her

hands and knees trembled. With annoyance or fear, she wasn't sure. She'd never been in a situation like this with Pat before. She expected him to be the one to check out any strange sounds for intruders. To protect her. To be the brave one. It was an old-fashioned school of thought, of course, but she expected it, nonetheless.

Trish paused at the top of the stairs and listened.

The scraping sound came from the cabinet. Now that she was closer to the source, it was more of a *thunk scraaaape.*

Trish turned on the lights. The sound stopped. She turned them off. The sound resumed. She flicked the lights back on and went into the living room. She grabbed the poker by the fireplace and held it in an attack pose, gripped the knob on the cabinet, and pulled it open.

The doll stood on the shelf, pickaxe raised. Small curls of wood decorated the shelf by his feet. On the inside of the door were long gouges dug deep into the finish.

Trish didn't know if it was because she was tired, having awakened from a deep sleep that way, or if her irritability toward Pat overshadowed any fear she had for the doll, but she picked him up by the arms and put him on top of the cabinet.

"I'm sorry," she whispered from the top of the stairs. Just in case. She flicked off the light. Before she made it to the bottom, she heard a thump from the upper floor. She closed her eyes and shook her head. Nope. Not going back up to investigate that.

When she climbed back into bed—sure to latch the bedroom door behind her—Pat rolled over and flopped an arm on top of her. She moved his arm away and curled up as far from him as possible in a childish attempt to make sure he knew she was mad, even though he was still asleep.

· · ·

Pat got up while it was still dark outside, the sun having not yet peeked above King mountain. He made a god-awful racket as he did so. Groaning and yawning loud and snarfing snot.

You shouldn't have drunk so much, she chastised him in her head.

"I'm going to make coffee." He announced it like she was sitting up bright-eyed and bushy-tailed, not curled up pretending to sleep.

The door to their room opened. His footsteps thumped up the stairs. All the while he yawned and groaned. Then he cried out. Trish snickered to herself. He must have seen the doll on top of the cabinet. Last he knew, the doll was inside.

He cried out again. "Trish," he yelled. Thwacking sounds followed by pained grunts followed.

Trish jumped out of bed. "Pat?" She ran up the stairs, slipping halfway and barking her shin on the wooden edge. At the top, she turned on the light.

Pat lay on the floor near the top of the stairs. Blood leaked from wounds on his torso. A gash across his neck spurted blood.

The doll stood next to his head. Kind eyes blankly staring. Rosy nose and cheeks suggesting his hidden smile.

Frozen mid-swing, the tip of its pickaxe was covered in blood.

Lucky, Magic, and Cotton Balls

He was a good boy, a loving boy. She saw it in him the moment she set eyes on him. Their bond was beyond any she'd had with any other living creature. She was glad her boyfriend—wealthy and married and unwilling to be a father to his lover's son—had left because there was no room for that lazy son of a bitch in her life now that she had Simon.

Over the years, there was a nearly imperceptible pulling away, so gradual, she didn't realize it until after his eighth birthday when she received the prints of their annual portrait together and compared it to the previous seven. In their first photo, he gazed at her with his one-year-old chubby face. Two, the same gaze with a wide-open mouth full of obvious delight. Three, a subtle shift away, a small smile pulling at the corners of his lips. Four, head tilted slightly down now with his eyes giving someone off frame a sideways look, the smile pulling at his lips but not yet exposing any teeth. Five through seven the shifts were even more subtle. The way he sat on her lap changed. First pressed back against her, until the eighth. Barely perched on her knee, toes of his sneakers touching the ground. He looked directly at the camera with a strange, secret smile. A knowing smile. And there was something in his eyes, in the way he held his head and looked directly into the lens, directly into the viewer's eyes.

"You're with him all the time," her sister said. "Maybe you should enroll him in public school and get some time to yourself."

What would she do with time to herself? How would she look after him if he were away from her? How would she know he was safe? She couldn't give up that knowing. Her sister—who had no children—couldn't possibly understand.

She found Simon out back in the patch of grass, shared by the adjoining townhomes, crouched with his back to her.

"Simon, honey, time for lunch."

He rose from a squat. There was something furry in the grass between his feet. When he turned around, blood covered his hands.

She stifled a scream and ushered him inside directly to the bathroom where she scrubbed the blood away and looked for bite marks or cuts or anything to tell her it was his blood and not the rabbit's. His skin was fiery red, and he had tears in his eyes when she finished.

"Did you … did you do that … kill … the rabbit?" Surely not. He was eight. Rabbits were too quick. He couldn't have caught it. She didn't press the question. She didn't want to know the answer, even though she already did, confirmed when he opened his mouth to speak again.

"I wanted to see what it looked like on the inside." His voice held no intonation. Flat and lifeless.

The next day, she took him to the public school down the street and enrolled him.

He didn't put up a fuss or show any emotion of any kind when she walked him to class and left him at the doorway. He gave her a half-hearted side hug and wandered off. Another boy showed him around the classroom.

She went home, poured a glass of wine even though it was far too early, and sank into sudsy bath water with a steamy romance novel.

But her thoughts kept wandering from the smutty book. Was he safe? Was he okay? Were the other kids being nice to the new kid?

His first day ended early.

"Your son," the teacher said. "Brought a rabbit's head to school." His tone implied she'd failed in her three years of homeschooling to properly socialize him. Like he was a puppy.

"Boys will be boys," she said with a laugh. "It won't happen again." *Because he's never coming back.*

That evening while she served dinner, she brought it up.

"Why did you take a rabbit head to school?" she asked him, scooping green beans onto his plate.

"I don't want to go back," he said.

"Answer my question." Her tone was sterner than she'd ever used on him. "Did you kill the rabbit?"

He nodded while shoveling food into his mouth and kicking his feet, his heels clunking against the rung under the chair.

He was out playing a few days later, and she went to gather his sheets for the wash. Something stunk. She followed the smell to his closet and to a box labeled "Lucky." Inside were dozens of rabbit's feet. Another box labeled "Magic" proved to be full of heads. Ears and all. A third box had "Cotton Balls" written on the top. She didn't look inside. She took them all and threw them away, stifling tears of horror.

"Lucky, Magic, and Cotton Balls?" she asked at lunch when she put his sandwich in front of him. For a second, a mortified look crossed his face, then he grinned.

"Lucky rabbit's feet," he said through a mouthful of bread and peanut butter. "Magicians pull rabbits out of hats by their—"

"Enough, Simon." She held up her hand to stop him. "Stop killing rabbits. It's wrong."

"But it's fun," he said like he was talking about playing tag with friends. "You should hear them scream."

The therapist came highly recommended. She took Simon on a Thursday after their math lesson at home. She'd briefed the doctor on the phone about the rabbits.

The session didn't go well. The doctor asked about Lucky, Magic, and Cotton Balls. Simon grinned at him.

"They're my pet bunnies."

"Simon, tell the doctor the truth," she said with a sideways glance at the doctor scribbling on his notepad.

The session ended with her screaming at her son, and the doctor prescribing her an anti-depressant.

"That was fun," Simon said in the car.

At home, she sent him to his room and poured herself a glass of wine. She tossed a pill back and chased it with a swallow of Cabernet, even though the label said to avoid alcohol while taking it.

Time disappeared, and she found herself slumped at the table and half the wine gone. She sat up, head groggy and full. The daylight had faded to full dark.

"Simon?" she called on her way up the stairs. Dizziness knocked her off balance. She fell against the banister and gave herself a few moments to get her bearings.

Simon laughed from somewhere in the dark. She couldn't see him.

"Simon? Where are you?" The words were slow and slurry in her mouth. She made it to the top of the stairs before she saw him there in the hallway. A little black figure gently illuminated by the bathroom nightlight.

He rushed forward and shoved her. She threw her hand out. It grabbed nothing but air.

The first hit was to the back of her head with a sickening crunch. She didn't feel the rest.

She came to at the bottom of the stairs. It was daylight. She couldn't move and her head hurt.

Simon shifted in her peripheral vision. He loomed his face over hers.

"You should have heard your scream, Mama," he said. "Let's see what *you* look like on the inside."

It was $800 for a tiny vial, but it promised "amazing results," as proven by several before and after pictures and time-lapsed videos showing wrinkled old women transforming into smooth-faced beauties.

Alexandra was skeptical. She was also nearing sixty and realized her husband had stopped looking at her the way he used to over a decade ago. He also didn't tell her she was beautiful anymore.

She rarely paid any attention to the kiosks that popped up in the middle of the mall walkway, but this one promising a fresh, younger look made her stop. And the fact that no one was hovering nearby trying to accost customers with free samples was a bonus.

"Hi there," a young saleswoman said with a bright and beaming smile on her tanned face. Perfect eyebrows. Perfect hair. She was probably in her early twenties.

"Hi." Alexandra moved to walk away but paused when the woman reached for her hand.

"I know what you're thinking," she said, an earnest

seriousness in her face. "There's no way this can work, right?"

Alexandra nodded. "I mean, sure, you can make your facial skin look younger, but your neck and hands will give you away."

The girl tittered. It was the only way to describe the sound and the way she held her hand—first hovering it over her ample bosom, then moving it in front of her perfect smile.

She leaned in. "You can put this stuff everywhere." She cocked a hip as if to say, even on your butt.

"Easy for you to say," Alexandra said with a smirk. "You're already beautiful. And all of, what, twenty years old?"

"I'm seventy."

"Bullshit." Alexandra covered her mouth at the involuntary exclamation. "Sorry," she said. "But that's absolutely ridiculous."

The girl could pull out her driver's license to prove it, but it could be fake. Like an employee badge that came with the job. Welcome aboard. Here's your new fake ID.

Instead, she pulled out her cell phone and showed Alexandra her time-lapse video.

"Could be edited," Alexandra said, but she'd lost any conviction in her voice as she watched the saleswoman's transformation.

Before she left the kiosk, Alexandra had dropped over two-thousand dollars on the tiny tube of product, the accelerator lamp, and the aftercare moisturizer. The saleswoman was kind enough to give her a free tote and several hand cream samples that were "the best moisturizers ever."

Not that Alexandra was naïve or gullible or anything like

that. In fact, she instantly felt buyer's remorse after she walked away. Hands sweating, shaking her head at herself, she almost turned around and went back, but talked herself out of it when she replayed the saleswoman's video in her mind.

The results would be nearly immediate. The time-lapse video took place over an hour's time.

Alexandra glanced at her phone. If she could get home in fifteen minutes, she would have enough time to get her first treatment completed before her husband, Ralph, came home from playing golf.

Excitement made her walk quicker to her car. He would shit when he saw her!

She made it home in twenty and got the lamp set up in the basement. It was a floor lamp that had a long arm at the top that illuminated a four-foot by two-foot area.

Alexandra wanted to focus on her face, neck, and chest for the first go. She smeared on the serum and lay down under the lamp on a blanket, naked to her waist.

An hour went by. Ralph still hadn't come home yet. Alexandra dressed, tucked the lamp away in a corner Ralph shouldn't have any reason to poke around in, and hurried upstairs. She closed her eyes when she went into the hall bathroom.

"Okay, here we go. Don't be disappointed if nothing happened. You can take everything back. Satisfaction guaranteed." She counted down from three and opened her eyes. She let out a faint cry and leaned toward the mirror, examining her face from every angle, touching the smooth and flawless skin. She'd never looked so amazing in her life. Not even when she *was* in her twenties and riddled with adult acne. She pulled her top down, exposing a pair of symmetrical and perky breasts.

The garage door opened. She pulled her shirt back in

place and bounced to the kitchen where Ralph would come in after parking the car.

The door opened, and Ralph—cheeks and nose slightly sunburned—stepped inside.

"Hey, Xandra," he said when he walked in, eyes on the floor. "What's for dinner tonight?" He bypassed her without looking at her and went straight to the fridge where he rummaged around and surfaced with a beer. Alexandra frowned. She didn't like the way he got sometimes when he drank. He cracked it open and took a long pull and finally noticed her. He barely stopped the beer from spewing out of his mouth.

"Who're you?" He took a step back into the refrigerator door.

"It's me, honey," she said. "I got some new skincare products at the mall today." She smiled. He gawped at her, eyes drifting to her chest. She pulled her shoulders back. His eyes widened, then sobered.

"Is this a joke?" He moved past her. "Xandra? Where are you? This isn't funny."

Alexandra frowned. She didn't look *that* different, did she? She followed him down the hall.

"Ralph. It's me. Ask me something only I would know."

He came busting out of their bedroom, visibly flustered.

"What's my favorite color?"

"Blue," she said.

"Ha!" He pointed at her. "No, it's green."

Alexandra huffed. "Well, it was blue last month when you insisted on buying that ridiculous espresso machine you have yet to use." She motioned toward the kitchen.

His mouth hung open then closed and opened again. His lips turned white.

"You said it was the same color as your first car. You forgot how much you loved it. The color, I mean." She put a sassy hand on her cocked hip.

Ralph pulled her down the hall to their master bathroom, where he turned on the light and examined her face with a clinical turn of her chin.

"I'll be damned," he said. "You look like a different person."

Alexandra glanced in the mirror. He was right. She didn't look like herself at all. Only her eyes. The color, not the shape or anything else. She looked almost like the saleswoman.

"Do you … Do you like it?" she asked in a nervous voice.

"I-I'm not sure. How long does it last?"

Alexandra hadn't asked but figured it was not a one and done situation. That would be a terrible sales model.

"You were—are—beautiful, inside and out. Why did you feel the need to do this to yourself?"

This was not the response Alexandra was expecting. She bristled.

"Because," she said, crossing her arms over her new boobs. "You stopped telling me. You stopped looking at me and noticing me, Ralph."

His shoulders drooped. He said nothing else, just turned and started the shower. He undressed without looking at her again and climbed in.

"Don't do any more treatments," he said. "I want my wife back."

Alexandra stormed out of the bathroom and sat on the edge of their bed. Mixed emotions flooded through her, mainly guilt at having spent so much. She should have just talked to him and told him how she felt, how she wanted him to make her feel.

She went to the basement and dialed the customer service number on the box.

"Are you unhappy with your results?" the customer service rep asked her.

"I'm happy … or I was … until my husband saw me." She cleared her throat. "He wants his wife back."

"Are you sure he's not just unhappy about the cost?" The rep laughed. "I'm kidding. You can return your products to the place you bought them from for a full refund. No questions asked."

"It's odd," Alexandra ventured. "I feel like I look just like the woman who sold this to me."

The rep laughed again. "Thank you for calling today. Is there anything else I can help you with?"

"No, that's all. Thanks." Alexandra hung up and repackaged everything as best she could. She hollered to Ralph that she was taking it all back. He yelled an affirmation that he'd heard her.

When she got to the mall, the kiosk was gone. Maybe they moved locations. She walked the entire mall looking for it, and when she still hadn't found it, she called the customer service number again.

"The number you have dialed is no longer in service. Please hang up and try again," came a robotic female voice, followed by three beeping tones. Alexandra dialed the number again and got the same result. She double-checked the number, a frantic pounding of her pulse making her hands shake as she poked the screen of her cell phone.

She made another lap of the mall, then stopped in the security office.

"There was a kiosk here earlier today—" she said. The security guard held up her hand.

"Ma'am, take a deep breath and calm down," she said.

I am calm, Alexandra thought, but her voice shrieked the words even inside her own head. She did what the security officer asked.

"Now, what can I help you with?"

"There was a kiosk on the stretch between Macy's and Sax," Alexandra said. "It was a beauty product kiosk."

The security guard nodded. "Okay," she said. "Do you have more information than that? A name? A description?"

Didn't the guard know what kiosks were in her mall?

"It didn't really have a name," Alexandra said, racking her brain. She looked in her bag. Even the box with the accelerator lamp and other products didn't have a brand, just the cutesy names of the products. Defeat started to wheeze into her chest.

"It was pink," Alexandra said. "The kiosk had a lot of pink and a TV playing videos."

The security guard didn't know of any kiosk that matched that description. She handed Alexandra a list of their current kiosks to see if she recognized any of the names, but she didn't.

"Thanks for your help," Alexandra said.

"For your information," the security guard said in her severe way. "You don't need any facial cream. Look at you. You're gorgeous."

Alexandra gave her a half-hearted smile and nodded. She shuffled out of the security office. Defeat was like a weight dragging her bosom to the ground.

"Hey," a voice whisper-yelled at her.

Alexandra lifted her chin and looked around.

"Over here."

She turned. A woman who looked just like Alexandra, and just like the saleswoman, but with light-colored eyes, stood in the entrance to the hallway for the bathrooms and payphones.

"You," Alexandra said, anger ripping her voice out of her throat. "You did this to me. I demand a refund."

The woman held up her hands. "No, no, no. You have it wrong," she said. "I know I look like the saleswoman, but I'm not."

"Yes, you are," Alexandra said. "You look just like her."

The woman shook her head. "Nope. Listen, you have to listen."

Alexandra didn't *have* to do anything, but she took a few deep—yet pinched—breaths through her nose.

"You got the same one as I did," the woman said. "I saw you come in with your bag, and I followed you until you went into the security office."

"That's not creepy at all," Alexandra said with a scoff.

"I bought this stuff a week ago." The woman pulled the vial from her purse. "I've been using it for over a month now. It only gets better and better. And by better, I mean worse."

Alexandra gulped.

"Let me buy you lunch, or coffee. Or a stiff drink." The woman left the hallway and ventured into the mall proper. Alexandra hurried after her, bag skimming the linoleum tiles. They ducked into one of the restaurants off the side near DSW and sat at the bar.

The woman ordered a glass of red. Alexandra ordered a white.

"You two sisters?" the bartender asked.

"Not even related," the woman told him with a wry smile. She turned to Alexandra. "Snacks?" She motioned to the happy hour menu. Alexandra shook her head.

"Tell me. Please. I just spent two grand on this stuff."

She nodded her head to the bag on the floor under her barstool.

The woman nodded. "I'm Patrice."

"Alexandra."

"I've been here every day for the past week looking for that goddamned kiosk, hoping some other unhappy soul would be by to make it reappear."

"What … what do you mean?"

Patrice let out a mirthless laugh. "Well, it's only there when it senses people need it, like when I run out and come here, it's there. Otherwise, it isn't. Or maybe I just can't see it." She shrugged. Alexandra scoffed. Patrice lifted her hands. "I know—I know. That sounds crazy. But hear me out."

Alexandra waited for the punch line. Their drinks arrived. Patrice took a hearty gulp of her red, and Alexandra followed suit. The Sauvignon Blanc she ordered was cool and crisp and exactly what she needed.

"I did some research online after I bought my stuff and basically did the same thing as you after reading reviews. The negative reviews I found were cagey and vague, almost like they'd had parts redacted or something. The positive ones were all peaches and cream, claiming it to be the best product ever."

Alexandra nodded along while Patrice talked.

"I found a blog, though, of a woman who had done a little more digging. She kept her post about the product high level—probably so the demons at the company wouldn't make her take it down. She said the same thing we're experiencing. She wrote about never seeing the kiosk until her bottle was empty. I emailed her to find out more."

Alexandra's throat had gone dry, and no amount of water—or wine—would rewet it.

"She gave me her phone number and told me to call her."

"Patrice, please. Get to the point. I'm sorry, but I need to know." Tears burned the back of Alexandra's nose.

"She said there are five types of products and depending on the salesperson who's at the kiosk when you go, that's who you end up looking like. There's a redhead, a blonde, a brunette, black hair, and that popular unicorn pastel colors hair. Even if your hair isn't that same color, it will be, eventually." She pointed to her head. "This used to be blonde." Tears welled in her eyes. "I used to look like my sisters."

Alexandra patted Patrice's shoulder.

"Why don't you stop using it?" she asked.

Patrice shook her head. "You don't want to do that."

"Why not?" Alexandra asked.

"Just trust me. You don't." She finished her wine and put a twenty on the counter. "Tell him to keep the change. I have to go."

They exchanged phone numbers and Patrice left.

Alexandra glimpsed herself in the mirrored wall behind the bar and did a double-take. Her hair, usually a natural gray shot with silver, looked different. It looked darker, almost. Less dimensional. She left the bar with her bag of products, did one more lap of the mall to no avail, and returned home.

Ralph was asleep on the recliner, mouth agape, and snores ratcheting from his throat. She took the stuff to the basement. When she reached the bottom step, she sat down hard and burst into tears.

"Why did I do this? What have I done?" She took the little box out of the bag and threw it across the room where it hit the opposing wall and landed on the floor. She didn't hear any glass break, but liquid oozed from the box. She covered her face and cried.

The next morning, her hair had turned completely brown from roots to ends and had grown substantially. She looked almost *exactly* like the saleswoman, except for the mole by her eye. A beauty mark inherited from her mother. Ralph had already gotten up and gone off to do God knew what, so Alexandra took a long hot shower. By the end, as she wiped the steam from the mirror, the beauty mark had vanished.

Don't stop using it.

Well, Alexandra's bottle was a greasy puddle on the basement floor, so she had to stop using it.

What would happen?

She got busy doing housework, occasionally leaning into the hall bathroom for a quick look in the mirror, just to make sure she still looked the same. Even her teeth had straightened and whitened, and her lips were red and shiny even though she hadn't put on any lipstick or gloss.

"What is this madness?" She smeared her hand across her lips to no avail. The color was just … there.

She texted Patrice: *Threw my bottle against the wall. Broke and spilled everything. How do I get more? You told me not to stop using it.*

The message showed delivered, but minutes ticked by with no response.

Just as well. Alexandra didn't want to use the stuff anymore. She just wanted her face back.

Twenty-four hours had passed since she'd done her first and only treatment. Ralph was still out, probably at the golf course again. She changed into a pair of sweatpants and a baggy shirt, an outfit that seemed to have fit her a little snugger the night before, and flopped onto the couch with a bowl of popcorn. She binged Queer Eye and fell asleep until the sound of a car door slamming woke her up. She looked out the front window just as a yellow cab pulled away.

Ralph stumbled in. Alexandra backed away from him.

"Well—hey there," he said, his eyes brightening without focusing altogether on her.

"Are you drunk on a *Sunday*!?"

"Poker night with the fellas." He belched meat and beer as he moved past her toward the kitchen. Alexandra followed him and stood in shock as he pulled another bottle from the fridge.

"No," she said. "No, you are done. You are already drunk. Put that back and go to bed." She would sleep on the couch tonight.

"Prettier wife, but still a nag." He listened, though, and put the beer back in the fridge. He gazed at her with glassy eyes and an inscrutable smile for a few beats, then approached her with his arms open and his lips puckered.

Alexandra hesitated but accepted his embrace, until Ralph's hands caressed her backside, and his slobbery mouth found her neck and her earhole. She backed away, but he held on. They bumped against the counter.

"Ralph, knock it off, I don't like this." He didn't stop. This was why she didn't like his drinking. Though she missed the attention he used to give her, this was not what she wanted. It was his gentlemanly ways, his tenderness. He'd always been a gentleman. Until he drank.

"Whassa matter?" He leaned away from her, stumbled back a step, but his hold on her kept him from falling. She gripped the counter to stop from being pulled down. "I thought this … I thought thisus whatchoo wanted."

Tears poured down Alexandra's face. She wrested

herself away from him and stormed down the hall. She slammed the master bedroom door and locked him out.

His footsteps made an uneven thumping down the hall. Something shattered on the floor, followed by his unintelligible muttering. He reached the door. The knob jiggled.

"Go away, Ralph," she yelled. "You're drunk, a-a-and I can't deal with you."

"Pretty lay-day," he slurred. "Let me in pretty lady." He tap-tap-tapped on the door.

Alexandra covered her ears and sobbed hysterically. "You're frightening me," she shrieked.

The sounds on the other side of the door stopped. Then his drunk singing started. He sang in German.

Alexandra climbed into bed and turned off the light, but she tossed and turned, replaying her conversation with Patrice, and what happened with Ralph over and over again.

Morning came too soon. Alexandra shuffled to the bathroom and sat on the toilet. She leaned her elbows on her knees and her face in her hands. She jerked upright and looked at her hands. They were normal … mostly. But her face, in her hands, felt soft and fleshy. She finished urinating and slowly looked in the mirror.

Alexandra screamed.

The face looking back at her wasn't human. It wasn't plant nor animal nor mineral.

It looked like her skin had melted and oozed down her face, leaving behind small openings for her to see out of. She thought her mouth was open from the scream, from the shock, but the draping balls of flesh hung down over it.

She lifted flaps looking for her mouth opening, her nose, her ears.

She ran a hand through her hair, and it came out in clumps. Alexandra screamed again. This had to be a nightmare.

Ralph pounded on the bedroom door.

"Honey?" he called. "Honey, what's wrong?"

He couldn't see her like this. He couldn't. She was a monster. Her tears got lost in the folds of skin. Her ugly cry face didn't even register on this hideous visage.

Her heart pounded, and she fought to take breaths that would fill her lungs completely. Then she remembered what Patrice had said.

Alexandra found a silk scarf in her panty drawer and wrapped it around her face.

"Ralph," she said, her voice blubbery behind the skin. "I'm coming out, but don't look at me."

"What's wrong, honey? Did you see a spider?"

Alexandra's hand shook as she reached for the lock on the doorknob. "Just … just don't look." Her voice came out a strangled whisper.

"Okay, I won't."

Alexandra unlocked the door and scurried past him. She grabbed her purse and jumped in her car.

She was desperate. An unhappy soul. The kiosk would be there. She'd buy another vial.

At the mall, she hurried inside, scarf still wrapped about her face so only her eye holes were exposed. People gave her strange looks, but she disregarded them.

The kiosk was there—between the Macy's and the Sax again. She all but sprinted to the counter, gasping for air behind her scarf and folds of flesh.

"Oh my," the saleswoman said. It was the same one from the day before. Or at least one who looked like her.

"I need another vial," Alexandra said. "I need … I need to be pretty again."

"I'm sorry, ma'am, but there is no way we can help you."

"Wha—What do you mean? I accidentally spilled my serum. There has to be a way."

The saleswoman cocked her head slowly to the side, shaking it back and forth in an oh-dear kind of way.

"I'm so sorry." She reached a hand toward Alexandra, then pulled it back and held it to her heart. "You are just too far gone." She shook her head sadly, *tsk-tsking*. "I'm so sorry."

Charles and Cori had just moved to the neighborhood. They hadn't met any of their neighbors officially yet but had waved to a few of them. Their waves were met with strange looks— who the hell was that? or do I know you? kinds of faces. Typical of the modern era when most people seemed to regard strangers with suspicion. Charles made a game of it.

"Wave super excitedly like you know them," he told Cori. "Neurotic smile, wide eyes."

Cori rolled her eyes instead. "Once they meet you and see your charming personality firsthand, they'll smile when they see us." She patted his hand.

"We'll see." He gave her a skeptical smirk.

At their old house, they were friendly enough, but whenever they had BBQs with close friends they'd known for years, those friendly neighbors would make a big deal of it. One time, Lee from next door just showed up, helped himself to a beer, and made fast friends with Charles's buddy from college.

It became a common occurrence. One day, Charles

noticed his buddy's unmistakable lifted Dodge in Lee's driveway.

It was the real reason he had looked for a new house, Cori knew, despite his objections when she brought it up. She could tell. She knew him. And when Cori got pregnant, they decided they needed more room, anyway.

A place with a bigger yard, a two-car garage, enough rooms for the baby, visitors, and Cori's studio. They found the perfect house outside town in the Friendly Mountain neighborhood. And, the best part, it was quite a few thousand under their budget.

For some reason, there weren't many offers on it. Charles checked Zillow only to see it had changed hands a few times over the past eighteen months.

"Something must be wrong with it," Cori said. But it passed all inspections. "Maybe someone died in there."

"No one died. They have to disclose that," Charles said.

Cori shrugged. She didn't know much about real estate stuff. That was Charles's skill set. As long as the house checked all the boxes for what they wanted and needed—it did and then some—she decided not to worry about why it was bought and sold so many times.

"Moving truck will be at the house by two." Charles reached across the console and placed a hand on the large swell of Cori's belly. "You and this bean just stay out of the way, okay?"

"I can help with light stuff," Cori protested. "I can't just stand around and watch."

"You tell us where to put everything," he said with a smile.

Because of her age—forty—and previous miscarriages, Cori was a high-risk pregnancy. Her doctor advised her to take things as easy as possible. But she hated feeling like an invalid.

"Find my studio stuff first so I can get to work again." She painted commissions for people. Portraits of beloved pets wearing sweater vests and glasses, smoking pipes, or wearing feather boas and tiaras looking elegant.

"Yes, ma'am."

They pulled up to the house, and Charles parked on the street out front, leaving the driveway for the moving van. They had some time to spare.

He got out and hurried around to Cori's side. He'd taken her doctor's orders super seriously and babied her every chance he got. Helping her out of the car was a little much, though. She smiled anyway and placed her hand in his.

The previous owners had done an excellent job cleaning before moving out. The place was pristine, as if no one had ever lived there. Cori and Charles had viewed —and smelled—so many houses trying to mask odors with plug-in air fresheners, and some that didn't try at all, as if to say, "yep, you'll have to replace all the flooring and paint or, you know, tear out the corners where my cat liked to pee." Nose blindness was obviously a real thing. That or people just didn't care.

The entry was one of the first things that attracted Cori's attention. Tall ceiling, and an open floor plan into the living room and kitchen. Stairs that turned back on themselves at a landing that overlooked the main living area. Her mind went through all their furniture, placing it around the spaces.

She moved into the room.

"Love seat here," she said. "That table we had in the hall should go there." She turned to Charles. "What do you think?" she asked. She dropped her arms. "Oh. You're doing it again."

"What?" Charles straightened from leaning against the wall. "Doing what?"

"Watching me 'dance through life'." She put it in air quotes.

"I never should have told you that." He caught her hand and pulled her against him. "But it's true." He kissed her. "Even with this belly, you move with grace."

He told her once it was a key physical trait that had attracted him to her at the very start, that she glided around as if life was a ballet.

"Would you rather I stomp around like an ogre?"

"It would help when you sneak up behind me."

"I don't sneak," she said. "You just don't hear me."

"Sneaking," he said in a low voice. He touched his nose to hers.

"Ahem." A voice cleared its throat from behind them, followed by a quick knock. Charles whirled around, taking Cori with him as if they *were* dancing. She struggled out of his hold.

"Charles Hill?" the man in coveralls asked.

"That's me," Charles said.

"Greg with Move It." The man reached out a hand. "We have your belongings."

"Groovy," Charles said. "You can back the truck into the driveway." They went outside, leaving Cori to her own devices. She spun in a circle—pirouetted, as Charles would say—and climbed the stairs to decide on which room would be the baby's, which her studio, and which one the guest room.

· · ·

They'd lived in the house for a couple weeks when things started happening. At first, a few items went missing. Cori blamed it on her pregnancy brain since it was only her things that moved or disappeared. In the back of her mind, she joked it was a poltergeist having fun with her.

A few commissions sat on easels around her studio. Three dog portraits and one cat. She had also started a triptych for the baby's room. She was about two days away from completing all of them when her tubes of black paint disappeared.

Charles was at work at a construction site, so she couldn't call him. She looked everywhere for more black paint. In her closets, still-unpacked boxes from the move, even in places she would never put tubes of paint—her underwear drawer, for example—just in case.

"Okay, Mr. Ghostie," she said. "I need that paint." She looked around the studio, up at each corner, suddenly feeling a strange prickle at the base of her spine. "Good job, Cori," she whispered. "You have successfully scared the shit out of yourself." She left the room, closed the door behind her, and went to the kitchen for a snack.

When she carried her plate and cup of herbal tea upstairs, the studio door was open. She paused, searching her mind for if she actually closed it or not. She knew she had because she'd scared herself and wanted to give the ghost an opportunity to return her paint.

Cori peered into the studio and dropped the plate and mug of tea.

The black paint had been returned, smeared all over her commissions, destroying them.

"No, no, no," she groaned from the doorway. She found the spent tubes on the floor, squeezed so hard they were twisted and misshapen. On the wall was a message.

"Welcome Home," it said in big scratchy letters.

Cold chased heat through her body. She backed out of the room as if the letters might jump off the wall and take chase. She closed the door and rushed down the stairs, swinging around the turn on the landing with a hand on the banister. She took the remaining steps two at a time in a mad dash to the front door. At the bottom of the stairs, she miraculously did not trip or slide out. She grabbed her purse and ran outside.

She called the police.

"There's someone in my house," she said, gasping and spluttering and talking so fast the dispatcher had to ask her twice to repeat herself.

"There's someone in my house," she said, slower now that she'd regained her breath. The dispatcher went through a list of questions and sent a patrol car.

After she hung up, she called Charles. He picked up. The sound of the construction site crashed and banged in the background.

"In the house?" he yelled into the phone.

"Yes. They stole my paint and wrote 'Welcome Home' on the wall in my studio." She burst into tears. "They ruined my commissions. All of them."

He stayed on the phone with her until the cops arrived, telling her it would be okay, her clients would understand.

Two officers went inside while Cori stayed outside with a third who questioned her.

"Black paint went missing," he said, scribbling in a notepad so quickly Cori wondered if he really was only scribbling.

"Yes, and someone defaced my paintings and wrote on the wall." Exasperation had crept into her voice. She wished Charles was there. He always kept her calm, just by his presence alone. He always said the right things, too.

The two officers came out.

"House is clear," one said. They proceeded to question her some more as if she were the one who'd vandalized her own studio.

"Did you see the writing on the wall? Upstairs? My ruined canvases?"

They had. But, since no one was there in the house, and Cori hadn't seen the perpetrator, there wasn't much they could do except have an extra patrol come by throughout the day.

"What about fingerprints? Take the empty tubes!" She flung her arms toward the house. The officer nearest her held up his hands placatingly, then motioned for one of the other officers to go back in.

By this time, dark clouds had collected in the west, looming and as uninvited as the looky-loo neighbors congregating across the street. It wasn't like the house was burning down. It was just a couple of cop cars.

Anger and annoyance started bubbling in Cori's veins.

They're just curious, she heard Charles's voice say in her mind. Followed by, *wave excitedly at them*. She felt better.

"Not first time, won't be last time," an accented and elderly female voice muttered.

Cori turned around to see an older woman shaking her head.

"Excuse me?" Cori said. The woman met her eyes.

"Oh, nothing," she said.

"No, what did you mean by that? Do you know something?"

The woman came nearer, tugging her cardigan tighter around her narrow frame.

"Previous owners, all complained," she said. "Complained of things happening." The woman gazed up at the house.

Cori looked but didn't see anything.

"What kinds of things?" she asked.

"Items disappear. Furniture moved. Messages. Cold drafts. Noises in the walls. Whispers." She whispered the last word.

Cori shuddered.

"Cops come. Never find anything to report. Promise more cars to drive by, but no one comes."

"Have you ever been inside?" Cori asked.

The woman shook her head. "Offered to. No one wants me in their homes."

Cori gave her a questioning look.

The woman pressed a hand to her chest. "I am a medium."

Cori nodded slowly.

"People don't believe, or they don't want to know the truth."

Cori didn't blame them, those who didn't want to know. But she *did* want to know.

"I can feel from here." The woman gazed at the house.

"What do you feel?" Cori asked, tugging on her necklace—a pendant shaped like an anatomical heart Charles had given her for Valentine's Day last year.

"Darkness."

The woman introduced herself as Silka and invited Cori to her house across the street. While Silka made tea, Cori looked around her living room, fascinated. Shelves lined one wall filled with crystals, bundles of sage and other herbs, and books about the occult, palmistry, and mediums. Various packs of tarot cards collected dust among small figurines and animal bones. Even a Voodoo doll; the pins in a small dish next to it. Cori grinned. There had to be something from every mythic culture collected here.

Over tea, they talked about Silka's gift. Cori had always been a believer but knew Charles would scoff when she told him about Silka. But she enjoyed listening to the woman's experiences.

"I feel presence and energy," Silka explained. "I sometimes smell or taste it at the base of my throat."

Cori avoided asking what the darkness was for as long as she could. Finally, she couldn't hold it back.

"What is it? The darkness you feel. About my house, I mean?"

Silka shrugged. "I only feel from outside. Must be inside to know more."

Before Cori could invite her over, her cell rang with Charles's ringtone.

"That's my husband." She thanked Silka for the tea and company. "Would you like to come over for lunch sometime?"

Silka followed Cori to the front door. "Perhaps."

Cori rushed across the street, waving to Silka from her front yard. The woman closed her door slowly. Cori went into the house.

"Charles?" she called.

"In the kitchen."

Cori went through the front room and down a short hall that opened on the kitchen, dining, and living room area. He opened his arms.

"What happened earlier? With the police?"

Cori filled him in. "They made me feel like I'd done something wrong by calling them," she said. Then she told him about Silka. She felt him tense when she mentioned Silka's gift. She pulled away.

"I know you don't believe in that stuff," she said. "But

I do."

Charles gave her a look that was half disbelief and half adoration.

"You don't want to have her over, do you?" he asked.

"Wouldn't you want to know if *someone* else was here with us? Another presence, I mean?"

Charles shrugged. "I would never believe that nonsense, so even if she said the devil himself was cohabitating, I would say the same thing. Absolutely not."

"Well, I'm sort of curious." Cori started pulling items out of the fridge for dinner. She didn't tell Charles that she'd freaked herself out before the paint went missing. If she did, he would absolutely not let her talk to Silka anymore. Or ever invite her over.

Not that he had that kind of control over her, or ever really exerted it. It would be more of a stern warning against it, knowing she'd do whatever she wanted anyway.

"I'm glad you made a friend of our neighbor," he said, ending all talk of Silka and her powers. They made dinner together.

That night Cori had a hard time falling asleep. Silka's voice saying, "Darkness," kept repeating itself in her mind, along with images of her destroyed paintings and the message on the wall. She'd have to contact her clients to let them know there would be a significant delay. She started drafting emails in her mind when she heard a bump from somewhere in the house, followed by scraping sounds.

"Charles." She nudged him in the ribs with her elbow. He grunted and immediately rolled over, snoring softly. She let out a huff and got out of bed. Under her side of the bed was a baseball bat. She pulled it out and settled it on her shoulder, hands choked up on the grip, prepared to swing, batter, batter, swing.

She crept down the stairs, ears tuned to any additional

noises. The scrape of what sounded like a chair on the hardwood issued from down below. Cori sucked in a breath. No voices or whispers. Just the occasional shuffling and bumping. Cori took the stairs at a sloth's pace, wanting and not wanting to see the source of the sounds. She pulled in a long and shaky breath.

"I called the police," she called down. "They are on their way, so you better leave."

The sounds continued as if she hadn't spoken at all. She reached the landing that looked out over the front room and flicked on the light.

A chair from the dining room slid across the floor, all four legs scratching the varnish on the wood. It slid to the front room where the rest of the furniture from the first floor was piled precariously like some kind of art installation at a museum. At the bottom was one of the other dining room chairs supporting a sectional, the dining room table, a large and unruly buffet table Charles inherited from his grandmother, a loveseat, two recliners, and everything else from the lower level. Even the silverware and stirring implements from the kitchen jutted out like porcupine quills.

Cori sucked in a breath when she saw her family's heirloom China set tucked here and there among the larger furniture. It all fanned upward into a conical shape, like a tornado. If she reached out over the landing, Cori could touch one of the bar stools jutting out from the side. If she wanted to. Which she didn't.

The chair got hung up on the rug and tipped forward, then flew to the top of the mass.

Cori backed away until she hit the wall. She let out a strangled and startled cry.

"Charles," she shouted. "Charles!" It came out as a

shriek. Thumping came down the hall as Charles pinballed toward her cry.

"What is it?" His face was pale. "The baby?"

Cori shook her head and pointed. Charles turned.

"What the—" He stumbled backward up two steps, then hauled Cori to her feet and dragged her back to their bedroom. Charles picked up the phone.

"Charles," Cori said, suddenly calm.

"Calling the police, gotta call the cops."

"Charles," she said louder.

He looked at her.

"What are the police going to do?"

"Someone did this," Charles said. He seemed to have forgotten the number for 911.

Cori shook her head and gently took the phone from him.

"I saw a chair," she said. "It was moving by itself."

Charles stared at her with a blank, uncomprehending face. "Chair?"

Cori nodded. "Moving by itself. No one touching it."

"Itself." He still didn't understand. "How are you so calm?"

Cori didn't know. Her stomach shook and her body felt riddled with chills. But seeing how Charles was reacting made her calm. Like she had to keep it together for the both of them.

"We need to call the police," Charles said, but his voice lacked vigor. Cori couldn't explain to him why it wouldn't help, but she knew it would make him feel better.

"You can call them, but they weren't helpful earlier, remember?" She handed him the phone.

"We can't stay here," he said. "They might still be in the house." He dialed, and the dispatcher answered before Cori could tell him there was never anyone there to begin with. She realized she was calm because seeing the chair move like that meant no human had been in the house earlier either. That's what had upset her the most about the paint.

A physical violation from a human seemed way worse than from—what? A ghost?

Darkness.

"We have to call Silka," Cori said.

Charles glared at her. "She did this," he said with zero justification. "To get you to buy whatever she's selling—yes I'm still here." He turned his attention back to the phone. "Yeah. Piled to the ever-loving ceiling." He got up and paced. "We need a patrol of the area, a search, we need to find these harassers! I *am* calm!"

Cori flinched. Charles waved his hands around exasperatedly. It was unlike him to be so enraged.

"I'm on hold. Again."

"Silka isn't selling anything," Cori said.

"We aren't calling her."

"You don't believe what I saw?" she asked.

Charles furrowed his brow.

"The chair? Moving by itself?" she reminded him.

He waved her off. "The lighting must have been bad."

"So, you don't believe me?" Cori ruffled. "I saw it fly to the top of the pile, Charles."

He didn't respond. Cori stomped out of the room. He yelled after her. She went downstairs, pausing on the landing.

The arrangement of the furniture was impressive. Cori didn't feel any ill energies, not that she was a conduit for that sort of thing. She reached out toward an eight by ten framed wedding picture and pulled it from the pile. It looked odd.

The entire funnel of furniture collapsed in a crash so

loud it muffled her scream. Charles flew out of their room and down to her, phone still against his ear.

"What the hell happened?" he asked, looking out over their damaged furniture.

Cori tried to explain, but the words wouldn't come out. Her heart hammered in her throat.

The photo. Someone scratched out Charles's eyes. No. Burned them. She handed the photo to Charles. He took it, his face paling.

"We can't stay here," he said. "Pack a bag."

Cori did. They were at a motel and checked in within the half-hour.

"Who would do this?" Charles asked no one. "Probably the same sick bastards who ruined your paintings." He wouldn't let her speak. She didn't care. He had to work through it in his own way. "First your paintings, and now this?" He waved the burned photo around.

Cori nodded.

"Sick sons of bitches."

Someone in the room next door pounded on the wall. "Keep it down in there," they shouted. Charles gave them the double bird.

As before, the cops were unable—unwilling, as Charles put it—to do much. Once again, they promised to send more patrols.

When Charles and Cori returned to the house, the front room was a disaster of wrecked furniture, and fingerprint dust covered everything.

A deep cold had enveloped Cori's heart. She hugged herself, wishing Charles would hold her. Instead, he moved around the pile of debris, huffing and making irritated grunting sounds.

Another three weeks passed. No new incidents, and their insurance agreed to pay for some of the damage to their belongings. No amount would replace her family's China, though.

Despite that, Cori looked around the front room, pleased with her design skills. It looked like Joanna Gaines from "Fixer Upper" had staged it. But part of her was still cold. She missed their old furniture. The couch they'd had since they first moved in together. She had talked about upgrading for some time, though, and this was the perfect opportunity. Silver lining.

Their life returned mostly to normal. Mostly. Charles became shorter with her more and more, almost as if he blamed her for what happened. He complained about work and the meals she cooked, calling her meatloaf—his favorite dish—inedible.

He started sleeping in the guest room with the excuse that he was having trouble getting and staying asleep and didn't want to keep her awake. But sometimes, when she got up in the middle of the night to pee, she could hear him pacing in there, grumbling.

Then the whispers started. Cori was working on a new painting. Having delivered the commissions only a week late, she could now focus on some personal pieces. She painted a unicorn portrait for the baby's room. After the triptych had been destroyed, she had lost heart in that project. She hummed a tuneless song while adding a few highlights to the horn and eyes. Someone whispered something behind her. She whirled around, but no one was there. She didn't know what they said. It was more the sibilant hiss of people whispering a few yards away, or through a cracked door. Like in a story she'd read about a man who got new ears that were haunted.

"Hello?" she called. "Is someone there?"

The sound stopped. She went to the doorway and listened. It came again, still too light to discern any words. Cori followed the sound out to the stairs to the landing. The sound was louder here, but still just hissing.

Cori went down into the front room, listening hard, and followed the sound to the center of the new decorative rug where the temperature dropped so severely, she gasped. Her breath fogged in front of her face.

She leaped over the other half of the rug toward the front door, her body trembling with cold.

A whimper escaped her.

The whispers came back. She inched forward, hand out. The cold was like a wall. The moment her hand touched the chilly air, the whispers ceased.

"Who's there?" she asked in a quiet voice. "Are you the ones who stacked the furniture?"

The whispers whispered faster. She stuck her hand through the cold wall.

An icy grip pulled her forward, then shoved her back out.

"LEAVE!" a voice growled.

Cori ran outside and across the street to Silka's house.

Silka opened the door before Cori even rang the bell and ushered her inside.

"Ramona, my spirit guide, told me we would have company today at this exact time," she said, smiling. But then she seemed to take in Cori's expression. She took Cori's hand. "Like ice. Let me make hot tea."

Cori had told Silka about the furniture shortly after that event. She told Silka what happened today while the woman put the kettle on.

Silka *tsked* while Cori told her story.

"The cold. Describe it."

"It was a wall. Almost physical, it seemed."

"And when you touched it?"

Cori had been cold since the furniture incident, so she told Silka about the whispers and the other voice. Thinking back, retelling what happened, she realized the cold wasn't a physical cold on her skin, like the chill of a winter day. It was deeper. As if her joy had been sapped away. In the moment she thought it was fear, but now she recognized it as some kind of absence. Like a hole in her being.

"I must go in," Silka said, rising. "I must learn what it wants, why it has targeted you."

Cori nodded. Charles didn't have to know. He wouldn't be home for a few hours yet.

Together, they crossed the street, and together they approached the front door. Silka took Cori's arm and a few times squeezed it and let out a small, pained groan.

Silka nearly dropped to her knees on the front porch.

"Are you sure?" Cori asked.

Silka nodded, her eyes full of tears.

Cori opened the door.

Inside, she still heard the whispers. "Do you hear them?"

Silka nodded and held up a finger. She closed her eyes. After several minutes, she opened them.

"They speak an ancient language," she said. "One so archaic it has been lost even to history." She turned to Cori. "The spirit tongue." She nodded her head. "Ramona tells me they speak of you."

"What do they say?" Cori asked, not sure she wanted to know.

Silka's lips formed a narrow line. "How is your husband?"

"He's fine," Cori said. "A little on edge since the furniture, like he's waiting for the people who did it to come back." Who was she kidding? There was more than that. She deflated. "Why hide it? He's different," she said. "He's … mean." Tears welled in her eyes. Silka patted her hand.

"The whispers are friendly," she said in an endearing voice. "They worry for you and your baby."

Cori looked toward the center of the room. "But … the cold …"

"The cold is not part of them," Silka said, her face darkening. "It is an outcast. A malignancy. A tumor on the heart of this home."

"The one who yelled?" Cori asked.

Silka shook her head. "The one who possesses your husband." Silka kept shaking her head slowly. "The cold inside you is a byproduct of the darkness sapping away the heart. You first noticed it after the furniture?"

Cori nodded.

Silka nodded along with her. She went to the door and beckoned Cori to follow. Out on the lawn she said, in a low voice, "We must rid the house of the darkness."

"How?" Cori asked, looking up at the second-floor windows for no reason at all.

"There are many ways in which to do this. Sage, priestly blessings, exorcisms." She waved her hand. "All well and good. But it must begin with you." She took Cori's hand. "You must remove your husband from the house. The farthest away you can get."

"He won't go," Cori said. "He's in the middle of a massive project. I hear about it every night."

Silka's lips formed a line again. "Then we must act quickly. You must fill this home with love. You must win your husband away from the darkness."

"I don't know how," Cori said. Despite his angry outbursts and hurtful comments and sleeping away from her, she'd remained civil, not letting her own frustration to light.

"You must love him. Continue to love him and show your love is ineffable."

Cori sighed. She had always believed the love between two humans to be conditional, rather than unconditional. Advanced thought processes, give and take, punishment, redemption, two wrongs making a right. All things that helped to satisfy love between two people. When imbalance was introduced, the seemingly unconditional love became conditional. Cori had justified all of Charles's actions, devising lies for him so she could live from day to day with this new, hopefully temporary, version of him. She hadn't realized how the cold in her heart had gone chillier in the past days, nor how her thoughts about him correlated. Until now.

She no longer smiled when she saw him. The thought of him filled her with dread, not love.

"The less love I feel from him, the less I feel for him, the colder my heart gets," she said.

Silka nodded.

"What do I do?"

"Only you know your own heart, dear," Silka said with a squeeze of her hand. "No one can tell you how to love another."

Cori escorted Silka back to her front door.

"I will concoct a tincture for your husband. Sneak it to him, for the darkness will recognize the scent of it and force him to reject it."

Cori nodded. "Thank you for your help." She hugged Silka, then walked back across the street to her house. She stood on the front lawn looking up at those windows again as if she might see someone standing there looking down.

Some manifestation of the darkness. It was hard to fight something she couldn't see. If she could hurt it …

"You must love him," she said to herself. And she knew she did deep down, but a person could only take so much.

She stood there with her eyes closed and let the sun warm her back. She dropped her hand to her expanding belly. As soon as she did, the baby kicked her palm. Cori cried out in surprise, then laughed. Her eyes filled with tears.

She ran inside and called Charles.

"What," he answered.

"The baby," Cori said, emotion making her voice waver.

"Oh god," Charles said. His voice softer, more … him. "Is he okay?"

"Yes," Cori cried. "Yes, he's okay. He just kicked me." She let out a sob of joy.

"Oh, Core," Charles said. "That's … that's amazing. I wish I could have felt it."

"You can. You will." The ice melted a little. "Can we meet for dinner? I can take a Lyft, then we can drive home together."

"Don't be ridiculous," Charles said, and for a minute, she thought he would burst into a tirade about saving money and how stupid she was. "I'll come get you."

They hung up without saying the usual I love you, but Cori was okay. He sounded like her Charles again, and she felt warmer inside.

An hour before Charles was due home, Silka came over to drop off the tincture. She said to empty the entire bottle into at least eight ounces of liquid, the stronger the liquid the better.

Cori got gussied up while she waited for Charles to come get her. She washed and curled her hair in a style he'd always liked, but she hadn't worn in a while. She put on a little extra eye shadow and a tinted lip balm. None of her clothes fit quite right with her expanded waistline, but she made do with what she had—a stretchy black t-shirt dress—making it fancier by accessorizing. She still felt like she looked like a toad in a circus tent.

Charles arrived. She headed out to the stairs, but when he slammed the door behind him, she halted in her tracks, heart sinking.

"Whoops, sorry. Didn't mean to slam it," he called up to her. Cori let out a breath of relief and went down to the landing. Charles looked up at her and smiled. "Wow."

Her heart warmed.

They went to their favorite place and had an amazing time. Charles was attentive and didn't talk about work at all. When he got up to use the restroom, Cori dug the tincture out of her handbag. She looked at it, considering whether or not she needed it. Cori pulled Charles's post-dinner whiskey toward her. It was far less than eight ounces, but she emptied the vial into it anyway.

Charles returned just as she put the empty bottle back in her purse. He downed the rest of his drink as he sat. After he swallowed, he made a sour face.

"Everything all right?" Cori asked.

"Yeah," Charles said. "I don't think I need any more to drink." He let out a laugh, but the mirth died on his lips.

The rest of the evening was beautiful. Cori felt like they'd erased the past few weeks.

When they got home and Charles climbed into bed with her, instead of in the guest room, and wrapped his arms around her, the chill seemed to thaw completely. His breath tickled the back of her neck as he snored softly.

Cori woke when the baby kicked her hard. Charles was gone, and his side of the bed was cold. It was three in the morning.

Thumps came from somewhere in the house. She climbed out of bed and peeked out into the hallway where residual light at the end of the hall illuminated the walls. Cori crept down the hall to the top of the stairs. She paused and listened.

Charles grumbled and muttered down in the front room. The thumping sounds continued, along with scraping and his occasional grunts. Cori took the first couple of stairs at a snail's pace. When she heard the crack of wood splintering, she rushed to the landing, still without a sound in what Charles would have said was sneaking around, and looked out over the front room.

Charles had the rug stripped away. It lay in a haphazard pile off to the side by the short hall to the kitchen. On the floor were a crowbar, a sledgehammer, and an assortment of saws and other tools. He'd pulled up one floorboard. The jagged edge of it jutted out over darkness.

Cori almost asked what he was doing, but he shifted, and the light hit his face. He didn't look like Charles. Ridges grooved his forehead, and his nose had an unnatural hook at the end. His skin held a strange and sickly pallor.

He grumbled, and the mutterings coming out of him were not his voice, nor any language Cori had ever heard before. Charles ripped up another floorboard.

Cori knew enough about house construction to know there should have been a subfloor under the thick hardwood slats with joists to support them. But there wasn't. Below, from her vantage point, was a dark hole. Like a physical thing, cold spilled out, frosting the edges of the broken boards. She could see it moving across the floor like a time-lapse of a pond icing over.

She had to get out of the house. But to do so meant getting past Charles and the cold.

Cori crept back to their room. She put on her sneakers and grabbed a light jacket from the closet. She pulled the baseball bat out from under the bed, then returned to the landing. The cold had nearly iced over the entire front room floor. It glistened in crystals on the furniture. Cori crouched at the top of the landing and peered down toward the short hall to the kitchen. She tossed the baseball bat down the stairs and into the hallway.

Charles jerked up with a startled sound. It might have been a word in the strange language. He stalked toward the sound to investigate.

The whispers—urgent—filled Cori's head. She took the stairs two at a time down into the front room. At the bottom, her sneaker hit the ice and her feet slid out from under her. She grabbed the banister, but her center of gravity was off because of her belly. She went down onto her tailbone.

She glanced down the hall. Charles was at the end, holding the bat. His back was to her. He hadn't heard her.

The whispers urged Cori on. She got up and skirted the edge of the room where the ice hadn't taken hold yet, though she could feel it coursing into her heart.

"Cori," Charles said from behind her. She was almost to the front door. The whispers stopped.

She turned. The ridges on his forehead and the hook of his nose were gone.

"Where are you going?"

"For a walk," Cori said. "I couldn't sleep with the racket you were making."

"Sorry," he said. "I have to uncover it." He was normal, but not quite. His eyes had a vacant look to them.

"Uncover what?"

He pointed to the hole in the floor.

"What is it?" Cori asked. Her heart pounded. She dared not glance to the door. She knew she had a dozen steps left before she could dash outside.

"His home," Charles said.

Cori gulped hard. "Whose … home?" her voice was barely a whisper.

The word he said was a series of strange sounds. Sounds she had never heard before. Sounds she wasn't sure a human throat or tongue could even make. She glanced at the dark hole, and when she looked up again, Charles rushed at her.

Cori jerked awake, this time for real. Charles wasn't in bed. A sinking feeling dropped into her gut and chilled the inside of her chest. She got up and listened at the door but didn't hear anything.

"Charles?" she called out into the hallway. The whispers started. Loud at first, then fading away as if the owners of the voices were walking away. Cori followed them to the landing, her mouth dry and knees weak and trembling. She looked over the rail.

Charles stood in the middle of the living room, back to the landing. Still like stone. A low growling purr filled the room with each inhale and exhale, matching the rise and fall of his shoulders.

"Charles?" Her voice caught in her throat.

"Charles isn't here." The voice was growly and echoed in her head. It came from everywhere around her. From inside her mind.

"What do you want?" Cori asked.

Charles turned and looked up at her, his expression pained. But it wasn't him. Not quite. Something was different in his face. Cori realized it was his eyes. They weren't Charles's eyes. She could see that. She knew his eyes. She loved his eyes.

"Love," the demon voice said. Charles's lips didn't move.

Cori flinched. Love?

"You … You shouldn't have made him mean then." She sidled down a few stairs, still holding the rail, still looking down at him. "You shouldn't have made it so cold." A couple more steps.

The demon turned, following her progress down the stairs.

"Fear and anger are the human's response," he said. "I do not create those actions."

"Your presence causes them," Cori suggested.

He seemed to consider this. Cori stepped down off the last stair, heart pounding. Charles was in there. She knew he was.

"You caused the cold," she said.

"A byproduct of the human's fear and anger."

Cori paused, one hand on the newel post.

"Let Charles back out," she said. "I love him. I can't love you."

The purring growl intensified. In a flash, Charles was in front of her, his face contorted in anger. A sneer pulled his lips back too far. Both upper and lower lips split in the middle. Blood dripped down Charles's chin.

"Stop," Cori cried out. "Don't hurt him."

His rumbling laugh vibrated in her chest. "A deal must be made," he said, turning on his heel and returning to the center of the room. "You cannot love me, you say, though I wear the face of your heart."

Cori's chin trembled.

"Perhaps he will love *you*, even if I am inside?" The demon cocked its head. "He will not know, after all."

Cori backed away toward the short hallway to the kitchen. The demon remained in the center of the front room where Cori knew the funnel of cold poured out of the floor.

"How does it work?" she asked, pausing. "Will I be me, if I willingly let you in?" A tear slid down her cheek.

The demon smiled and nodded. "We can coexist."

"And once you get what you want? Once you feel love, will you leave? Will you be satisfied?"

The demon nodded slowly.

Cori dropped her hand to her bulging belly. More tears dripped from her chin. "And my baby—" she gasped. "My baby will be okay?"

He nodded again.

"Okay," she said. She took a deep breath. "Okay."

The demon held out his hand. Cori held her breath and clamped her lips together and went to him. She did not take his hand.

"A deal is made with the clasping of hands," the demon said. "And a kiss to transfer." He raised his eyebrows.

Cori looked into his eyes, into Charles's eyes, but not quite. She did this for him, to save him, because she loved him. She wanted him back the way he was, when she used to catch him watching her with adoration and that stupid smile she loved so much.

She lifted her hand and placed it in his. He pulled her close and kissed her.

There was no pain, just a trailing of ice as the demon

slid from Charles into her. It coursed down her throat and into her chest where it pulsed with the beat of her heart, then slowly subsided as it sank lower to her stomach, and lower still to her womb. She jerked away.

"No, no!" She clawed at her skin, trying to stop the demon. "That wasn't the deal," she shouted. The laugh reverberated in her mind, then diminished.

Charles dropped to his knees with a gasp and a series of coughs. Cori kneeled at his side. He grabbed for her, clinging and drowning in whatever the demon left behind. A vacancy, maybe, in his chest. His lungs expanded to their full capacity. She helped Charles to his feet and pulled him out of the funnel of cold. His legs wouldn't hold him, and he collapsed again in the kitchen hallway, pulling her down with him.

"Cori?" Charles said in a choked voice.

"I'm here." Cori held his face between her hands. She pressed her forehead to his.

"What happened?"

"You … You had a bad dream. You were sleepwalking." The lie slid too easily off her tongue.

"You were crying," he said, wiping the tears from her cheeks.

"I was scared," she said. "But now I'm okay." The baby kicked. She lifted Charles's hand and pressed it against her belly. "Feel."

A look of concentration fell over his face. The baby kicked again, and Charles grinned and let out a breathy laugh.

"Oh my god," he said. "That's amazing. Let me feel again." He wrapped his free arm around her and together they sat on the floor feeling the baby kick.

Feeling the demon yearn to feel their love.

Acknowledgments

I would like to thank the following people for helping to make this book possible:

My beta readers: Michael F. Haspil (author of *The Graveyard Shift)*, Amy Drayer (author of *Revelation*), Amanda Keil (one of my dearest friends), and Melissa McMurphy (my universe twin who makes me laugh almost daily). Thank you for the amazing comments and suggestions to take this book to the next level!

My editor, Stephanie Kleewein of Stephanie Kleewein Communications. Your edits reminded me why I really do need an editor. Thank you for your keen attention to detail!

My sister, Melissa "Wissa" Sirevog, and Tim White for helping make "A New Set of Ears" less confusing (maybe).

My husband, Tim, for massive amounts of support and for keeping me alive for the past 14 years.

And Kira, who reminds me to find joy in *everything*.

About the Author

Claire L. Fishback lives in Morrison, Colorado with her loving husband, Tim, and their pit bull mix, Kira. Writing has been her passion since age six. When she isn't writing, she enjoys drawing, reading, hiking, baking, and adding to her bone collection, though she would rather be stretched out on the couch with a good book (or poking dead things with sticks).

Please visit www.clairelfishback.com and sign up to stay up to date on the latest releases and more!

If you enjoyed *The Doll Room*, you might also enjoy *Lump: A Collection of Short Stories*!

www.ingramcontent.com/pod-product-compliance
Lightning Source LLC
Chambersburg PA
CBHW021140190726

48288CB00008B/2743